IT IS ENOUGH!
FINDING PURPOSE IN SUFFERING

Lawrence Bowman

WAYMAKER PUBLISHING

IT IS ENOUGH!
FINDING PURPOSE IN SUFFERING

All scripture quotations are taken from the King James Version (KJV) of the Holy Bible.

ISBN- 978-0-9988869-9-2

Printed in the United States of America

A special thank you to Joshua Rivedal for his assistance with the editing of this book.

For information about special discounts on bulk purchases, please contact the author.

Follow Lawrence Bowman on Facebook.

Explore more inspiring content from Lawrence Bowman at www.MissionFrontier.info/blog and discover additional books at www.MissionFrontier.info/books.

CONTENTS

DEDICATION

After my book *Confessions: A Memoir of Hope for the Suffering* was published in 2024, emails, social media messages, texts, and phone calls began to find their way to me, from across the United States and far beyond its borders. Each voice carried a story. Some wrote of pain and loss, while others expressed doubts that they had long been afraid to share. Many simply sought to ask questions about God, questions that had lingered quietly in their hearts for years.

Each time someone reached out to speak with me in confidence, to share something they had never shared before, I was deeply moved. Their honesty and courage stirred me to seek the LORD more earnestly, and over time, their words compelled me to write. Yet as I sat down to begin this book, I knew I didn't want to write another "help" book or a weary account of suffering. My desire was purposeful. I longed to write each page from the depths of my heart, as though I were sitting across from you, having a heart-to-heart conversation. As I wrote, I imagined us speaking openly about our sufferings, our questions, struggles, doubts, and fears, and most of all, listening together to what the LORD says in His Bible about the pangs that weigh upon our hearts.

I dedicate this book to each of you who have entrusted me with your stories, your pain, and your faith in God. Your courage, your questions, and your openness have been a source of inspiration for me. You are the reason God has given me the privilege of writing these pages. My prayer is that, somewhere within these words, one more heart bewildered by suffering will find hope, comfort, and understanding in Christ Jesus.

Thank you,

Lawrence Bowman

For our light affliction, which is but for a moment,
worketh for us a far more exceeding and eternal weight of glory;
—2 Corinthians 4:17

PART I

Understanding Suffering

--- 1 ---

WHEN
THE ACHE IS PERSONAL

Is suffering good? Some will tell you it is, that it is not only good, but a hidden treasure, a gem we are meant to cherish. But how can that be true? How can something we hate, something that breaks us, that steals our sleep and gnaws at our hearts be good for us?

If you have ever felt that ache in your chest, or the hollowness of a life disrupted by loss or pain, you know the answer feels impossible. And yet, it is a question we cannot escape.

I know that ache intimately. There is a kind of pain you do not speak of, and it is not because you are hiding. It is often unspeakable because there are not enough words to comprehend it or explain it. I have been there. I still carry painful memories laced with confusion, my innocence stolen, and shame pressing silence over my mouth. For years, I carried that ache in the dark corners of my heart, hoping no one could see.

But pain has a way of finding us again, just when we think we are safe. I first heard its haunted hush in a hospital waiting room as a teenager. The silence felt thick in my chest, and the dread of waiting filled the air under the hum of sterile fluorescent lights. Shoes pacing linoleum. Prayers cried into air too thin to hold them.

A loved one had been shot in the head. The bullet tore through one temple and out the other. I stood stunned, surrounded by family, too shocked to cry. For days, then weeks, we held our breath, bracing for whatever might come. Hope felt fragile. Time blurred... but pain did not.

Not all suffering screams. Sometimes it whispers, slowly eroding the life you've built until one day, it is simply gone.

I remember, as a young adult, handing over the keys to my home. The foreclosure was final, but the despair had arrived long before. Walking away meant more than losing a home. I left stability, rest, and the place where dreams once lived. I didn't know where I would sleep next, or how to tell anyone. I only know that I locked the door one last time, placed the keys in the banker's hand, and pretended I still had somewhere to go. Inside, I felt hollow and paralyzed. It was as if life was unraveling while I watched from the outside.

I have seen suffering up close, which is why the pages in this book are not theory, a ten-step recovery guide, or a lecture on why hardships happen. It is a journey carved by wounds, shaped by questions I have asked, held by the God who met me in them, and the sustained hope I have found along the way.

We are living through historically difficult times, and many hearts are carrying more than they know how to express. Maybe you are on a similar path. If you have ever wondered where God is when everything falls apart… If you have ever sat alone in the dark, asking, "Why me?" If you have ever suffered in secret, too afraid to tell your story, too wounded to believe it still matters… Then this book is for you.

I do not write this as someone with all the answers. I write as someone who has been in the pit of shame and despair, covered in ashes and rubble. Yet somehow, through it all, I have discovered a God who draws near, even in our deepest pain—a Saviour who meets us at our lowest and refuses to walk away. A Saviour who does not ignore suffering, but transforms it.

This is the story I want to tell you. And it is not only my story; it is all of ours.

WHAT WE ALL CARRY QUIETLY

I wish I could sit across from you as you read these words, because if I could, I would look you in the eyes and say: I don't know what kind of pain you've faced, but I know what it means to hurt.

I wonder about you, the questions that rise when the house grows silent, when the funeral ends, when betrayal cuts deep, when friends stop calling, or when the prayers you have cried seem to go unanswered. Those questions live close to the heart. And if you have asked them, you are in good company. I want to walk with you through those places so we can discover together what God is doing in the middle of it all.

Part of walking gently with others is remembering that we never fully know the weight another soul is carrying. Only they know how deeply they are being stretched. That is why I try to speak with care when someone entrusts me with their pain.

For some, their pain lies in the grief of losing someone beloved. For others, it is the pull of anxiety that never loosens its grip, or the disloyalty that shatters trust and bruises the spirit. Some carry chronic pain that gnaws at their strength day after day. Others suffer in silence, invisible to the world, but not to God.

Whatever form it takes, suffering is a universal part of the human story. It reaches every heart, every home. And when it strikes, one question always rises: *Why?* Why does God allow suffering? What good could possibly come from all this?

These are not abstract questions. These are questions I have wept through, wrestled with, and carried into sleepless nights. And I know I am not the only one.

After many years in ministry, walking alongside countless people whose lives are filled with grief and heartache, I have learned one thing for certain: suffering never stays far away. It does not wait for an invitation. It barges in, unannounced, and eventually visits every doorstep. It has visited me more times than I care to count.

Much of my story is already out in the open. In *Confessions: A Memoir of Hope for the Suffering*, I share seasons marked by betrayal, injustice, physical agony, and devastating loss. Yet through every heartbreak and every lonely night, one truth has never failed me: the comfort of God's Holy Bible. When nothing else made sense, and no answer came, Scripture did what it always does, speaking life into death and peace into the storm.

Passages like 2 Corinthians 1:3-4 have become an integral part of my testimony: *"Blessed be God, even the Father of our Lord Jesus Christ, the Father of mercies, and the God of all comfort; Who comforteth us in all our tribulation, that we may be able to comfort them which are in any trouble, by the comfort wherewith we ourselves are comforted of God."*

I have felt that comfort up close and personal; it has been my lifeline. And now, my heart is to come close to you in your crisis. I believe God has called me to extend the same comfort I have received, to meet you where you are, and to say: You are seen. You are remembered. And you are never beyond redemption.

THE UNIVERSAL QUESTION: WHY?

Suffering cannot be solved with quick fixes or oversimplified answers. And I want you to know that I am not here to hand you a cliché or patch a wound with empty words. I won't insult your pain by saying, "It's just part of life" or "God has a reason." You and I both know that when the storm is raging, those words cut more than they comfort. Pain is too real to be explained away.

When you're deep in it, logic does not help. Your body aches, your heart feels like it is about to burst. You have no song, and even your prayers seem to hit the ceiling and fall back down. You don't want a theological lecture. You want to know someone sees you. To know God has not turned His face away.

And in moments like that, sometimes, it's not about understanding the pain; it is about knowing you are not abandoned while experiencing it.

Even Scripture, when tossed out carelessly, can feel like a slap in the face. Maybe you've been there, broken and trembling, and someone quotes Romans 8:28 (you know, *"all things work together for good..."*) at you like it's a bandage. And instead of bringing peace, it is suffocating.

Here is the good news: Jesus never treated suffering lightly. He did not toss out Scripture like aspirin. He stepped into suffering Himself. He walked straight into the fire *for* us and *with* us.

Hanging on the cross, beaten and bloodied with lashes cut to the bone, Jesus cried out, *"My God, my God, why hast thou forsaken me?"* He was entirely God, fully human, hanging between Heaven and Earth, breathing agony and exhaling anguish. His flesh had been torn open. His hands and feet were pierced. But it was more than physical pain. It was the weight of becoming all of humanity's sin, the despising shame, and the agony of being forsaken by the Father, all bearing down on Him at once. And He chose to experience that for *you*.

So, when you cry out and wonder if anyone understands, you do not have to look any further than the cross. There, Jesus did not merely speak about suffering—He embodied it.

And the cross was not an isolated moment; it was the culmination of a life marked by suffering, humility, and love. Before His death and resurrection, He lived among the poor. He was misunderstood and overlooked. He had no place to lay His head, no position in society, no army to defend Him. His friends often failed Him. His enemies hated and reviled Him. And yet, He kept loving. Kept walking. Kept giving.

He was, as the Prophet Isaiah said, *"a man of sorrows, and acquainted with grief"* (Isiah 53:3).

So when you ask God, *"Why,"* He does not rebuke you for asking. He does not demand we hold it all together. Instead, He invites us to bring our doubts and broken questions to Him. He meets us there, not always with immediate answers, but always with truth and love.

God may permit what He hates in order to accomplish what He loves. Knowing this, I have come to believe with all my heart that your suffering is not meaningless. It may feel random. It may seem cruel. But God never wastes it.

You may not see the whole picture right now. You might be living in a season that feels chaotic. But there is an Author at work. One day, you will look back and realize that God was doing something sacred in your sorrow. He was building your trust, deepening your faith, and forming something in you that could not be done any other way.

So, before we ask why suffering exists, let's anchor ourselves in the fact that we are not alone. Jesus meets us in our lowest pits. Not with lectures, but with love. He enters the pain, walks through it with us, and slowly turns it into something filled with meaning and purpose. This is the foundation we must stand on before exploring the deeper questions of sin, sorrow, and redemption.

So, take a breath with me, and let's keep walking forward.

2

THE BROKEN BEGINNING

There is something inside us that knows this world is not how it is supposed to be. We see it in nature. We feel it in hospital rooms and at funerals. It's in empty chairs and broken relationships. It fills the headlines that make our hearts ache. Deep down, we know we were made for more than this—and we are right. Because the world, and mankind, did not start out this way. The Holy Bible does not open with tragedy. It opens with beauty.

In the first pages of Scripture, we find a world untouched by grief. There is a garden, and within it, there is harmony, intimacy with God, and creation at peace. In the Garden of Eden are two individuals made in God's image, formed with purpose, dignity, and love. They walk in perfect fellowship with their Creator. There is no fear, no shame, and no suffering. Only goodness. But it did not last. And that is the part that hurts.

They were not scripted beings, acting out a predetermined role. These two people had the capacity to choose. And in the beginning, all they knew was goodness. But that peace was fragile. There was only one boundary. One tree. One command to protect them.

And yet, like us, they were drawn to what was forbidden. Tempted by the serpent's lie that they could be "*as gods*," they reached for more and lost everything. In that one moment when they abandoned their trust in God, everything else broke too.

Pain entered the world like a torrent. Not just physical pain, but soul pain: separation, shame, fear, and death. And it has been rippling through every generation since.

A BROKEN WORLD

Suffering did not sneak in while God was occupied. It came in through the front door, invited, not by God, but by us.

It exists for a reason, and at the root of it all is something we do not like to talk about anymore: *sin*.

I know. It makes many people uncomfortable. It is unpopular. It sounds harsh, even outdated. That word *sin* conjures images of condemnation, guilt, and judgment. But if we are going to talk honestly about suffering, we have to name its source. Because if we do not understand what broke the world, we will never understand why it hurts so much or why we desperately need hope.

Suffering entered the picture the moment humanity stepped outside of God's perfect design. Genesis 3 tells the story. Adam and Eve, living in perfect harmony with God, chose to believe a lie. Instead of trusting the One who created them, they reached for control: grasping for independence. They wanted something they already had: likeness to God. And in that one moment, the sacred shattered.

From that day on, sin and death became part of the human experience. Not because God desired it, but because love cannot be forced. God could have created a world where obedience was automatic, where devotion was hardwired and loyalty guaranteed. But compelled love is no love at all. Real love involves risk. The risk that we would turn away. That we would reject His goodness. That we would choose our own way, and break the world He gave us.

And we did.

At its core, sin is simply living outside of God's design. It is the moment we choose our own desires over God's commands. It is saying, "I'll do it my way," even when God's way has been lovingly laid out for us.

Sin does not always look like a dramatic, earth-shattering act. Sometimes, it is subtle, an unnoticed failure to choose what we know is right.

If we're honest, we have all been there. We have all chosen our way over God's way. Even if we have never committed what many call "major sins," we have all fallen short. Every one of us. Me included.

It is easy to look at the pain in the world and point fingers. We blame politicians. We blame systems. We blame each other. But the truth is harder to swallow: sin lives in me. It lives in you. It lives in all of us.

We see it in small decisions: when we choose comfort instead of compassion, justify shortcuts, ignore the hurting neighbor, or scroll past the suffering stranger online. And those small choices, multiplied over generations, have produced a world fractured and groaning under the weight of its rebellion.

The Apostle Paul captured it like this in Romans 8:22: *"For we know that the whole creation groaneth and travaileth in pain together until now."* That's the world we live in, a creation still reeling from Eden's loss.

But here's the mystery that haunts many: Why did God allow this? Why didn't He stop it? Why let sin take root at all? Theologians have wrestled with those questions for centuries. And while we may never fully grasp all the layers, Scripture offers something breathtaking: God wanted us to love Him freely, not out of force or fear, but from the heart.

Love, to be genuine, must be chosen. And because God longed for a relationship and not programmed obedience, He gave humanity the gift of freedom. With that freedom came the possibility of sin.

Yet even in the fallout of disobedience, God did not turn His back. He stepped in, offering us mercy. He did not create suffering, but He redeems it.

Our world may be broken by death and decay, but we are not without hope. Not because we feel strong, but because God is still sovereign. Even when it seems like everything is collapsing, He is still working, especially in the places that hurt the most, to bring about good we cannot yet see.

THE NATURE AND CONSEQUENCES OF SIN

Sin not only affects us personally; it sends shockwaves through everything and everyone around us. It wrecks relationships. It erodes trust. It distorts the way we see God and how we view others. It twists our understanding of who we are and what we were made for. We often think of sin as just "bad behavior," but it runs far deeper than that. It is not merely a list of wrong actions; it is a breach in the soul. Sin is a condition, like a gravity that pulls our hearts away from truth, joy, and the God who created us.

When we're caught in sin, we are like a fish tangled in a net. We thrash, fight, and try to free ourselves, but the more we struggle, the tighter it wraps around us. We panic, lose perspective, and slowly forget who we are, until we no longer remember who we were created to be.

Sin does not just separate us from God; it undermines our very identity. It clouds our judgment. It twists our desires. But the worst part is that it convinces us that emptiness is normal. Yet, we were designed for joy that runs deeper than circumstances and for purpose that outlasts pain.

But when we live in sin, we live far beneath our design. We become disconnected from the One who gives us life. That is why the consequences of sin are deeply personal. They touch our emotions, our decisions, our health, our families, and our future.

Scripture does not sugarcoat it. Romans 6:23 tells us: *"For the wages of sin is death."* Not only the death of the body, but the loss of peace, joy, and the fullness of life we were meant to experience.

It's a slow unraveling. A gradual drifting away from the abundant life God longs to give us. Most people do not realize it's happening until they wake up one day feeling empty, angry, bitter, or lost.

That's what happened in Eden. When Adam and Eve turned from God, everything changed. The ground was cursed. Pain and death entered time and space. What was once whole became fractured. And that brokenness did not stop with them; it spread to every heart and every generation.

The suffering we see today is not random or circumstantial. It is systemic. It is the spiritual fallout of stepping outside God's design. But here's the part that stops me every time: even in all this ruin, God did not walk away. He could have. He had every right to abandon the world we damaged. But instead, He chose to step into it.

This is where the story turns, where death does not get the last word, where sin does not have to lead to destruction, and where guilt does not have to become your identity.

This is where redemption begins, not because we deserve it, but because Jesus came for us.

THE GOOD NEWS HIDING IN THE RUINS

God did not leave us in our separation. From the moment Adam and Eve fell, He began unfolding a plan to both forgive sin and defeat it. A Saviour would come—God Himself.

That Saviour is the Lord Jesus Christ.

When God chose to enter into creation as a human being, He did so in the most unexpected and unlikely way imaginable: with humility. Rather than appearing as a mighty, untouchable deity or following the patterns of gods in myths, spoiled and detached, He entered the world as a tiny, helpless baby in a dirty stable.

As He grew into manhood, He did not pursue worldly power, indulgence, or comfort. Rather, He lived a life of quiet ordinariness, moving among the overlooked, the outcast, and the riffraff of society. He spent most of His ministry in small towns and rural areas, far from

Jerusalem (the seat of political and religious power at the time), until His time came to offer His life.

When that time arrived, Jesus did not attempt to seize power from the Pharisees or violently overthrow the occupying Romans. Instead, He willingly subjected Himself to deprivation, ridicule, false accusations, and malicious rumors that branded Him as a glutton, a drunkard, a friend of sinners, and even an imposter. Then He laid down His life as a ransom for His enemies, sinners like us. He did not just endure suffering; He became its embodiment.

He did not simply record the debt of our condemnation and leave it unpaid. He drove every accusation into the wood with the nails that pierced His bloody body. What He did on the cross was permanent. Finished and paid in full.

So, if you feel the weight of guilt, shame, or separation, lift your eyes. Look to the One who made you. In Christ, you'll find a love deeper than shame, stronger than sorrow, and more faithful than your failures.

The cross was where God met humanity in a way He could nowhere else. Full satisfaction. Full peace. No more separation.

It is this very truth that enables the Christian to rest in Christ, to trust in His care, and to find peace in His presence. In Christ, we discover a life of confidence, knowing that He who suffered for us also walks with us through every sorrow.

This is the beauty of the Gospel: while we were yet sinners, Christ died for us. He did not wait for us to clean up our mess or get it all together. He came to us in our brokenness, our sin, and our hopelessness, and offered a single, for all time solution we could never resolve ourselves.

And this reframes how we view suffering altogether: Jesus chose suffering, both in how He lived and how He died. He did not avoid it or pass it off onto others. He did not use it to advance an agenda. Instead, Jesus deliberately chose a life of humble discomfort and physical agony.

What does that say about how life should be lived? What does that say about our modern existence with all its comforts and securities?

THE PURPOSE OF SUFFERING

If God dealt with sin at the cross, why do we still suffer?

If Jesus won the victory, why does life still feel like a battlefield? Why do the aches linger? Why the diagnoses, the betrayals, the losses?

The short answer is that God is still working. He did not merely save us *from* something; He is saving us *through* something.

Suffering, in the hands of a wise and loving God, becomes the very tool He uses to reshape us. It is part of how He loosens what binds us and leads us into what sets us free. It is not pointless. Suffering is not God's punishment, nor is it a cruel game. And it is not something we grit our teeth to simply "get through." No struggle is random. Each one is part of the refining process, shaping us into the people God is preparing for what lies ahead.

And if I can say this plainly: more often, suffering works like a careful scalpel God uses to sanctify and cleanse us from the hidden layers of sin that hold our hearts captive. Through suffering, the distractions that once consumed us begin to lose their grip, and we discover that only God remains unshaken. It is in this stripping away that we learn that true living is walking closely with Him, embracing His purpose, and reflecting His love.

But to be honest, that fellowship is rarely marked by ease. More often, it unfolds in seasons of hardship. God loosens our grip on worldly comforts to awaken a hunger for what is eternal. The very trials we would avoid often become the doorways that lead us deeper into His presence.

We long for mountaintop experiences, for a faith that soars beyond the ordinary. We admire those who seem to walk with God in radiant intimacy. But what we often miss is that the path upward usually runs through valleys. Growth doesn't happen without sweat, tears, and fire.

Every trial, tear, and affliction becomes part of the slow work God uses to refine our faith and teach us to depend on His strength instead of our own might.

The psalmist said it best: *"My flesh and my heart faileth: but God is the strength of my heart..."* (Psalm 73:26). It is often in the moments when we are most undone that we discover God is most near.

And His comfort is as tender as a mother soothing her child, and as strong as the everlasting arms that hold us. As He promised Israel, the same assurance extends to us: *"As one whom his mother comforteth, so will I comfort you"* (Isaiah 66:13).

And here's the wonder: that same comfort doesn't stop with us. It equips us to comfort others.

I've seen it in my own life. The places of deepest pain have become the places God uses most to soften my heart. They have trained my eyes to see what I would have overlooked. Shared suffering becomes a bridge. It dismantles walls. It lets us sit with another soul and say, "I've been there too."

That is precisely what Christ did for us.

Now, when we walk through valleys, we do not walk alone. And when we meet others in theirs, we can extend a compassion forged in the fire of our own pain. That is the beauty of this journey: God does not waste a single wound. In His hands, even the deepest suffering can be transformed into a vessel of grace.

But if we're going to understand suffering fully and how a good God can allow it, we need to trace the story all the way back to where it began.

3

GOD'S REDEMPTIVE PLAN

To truly understand suffering, not just intellectually, but deep in our hearts, we have to begin with the fact that God is sovereign. That means nothing takes Him by surprise. Not even a diagnosis, grief, betrayal, or the days when you feel like you're barely hanging on. He is still in control, even in the waiting. His sovereignty is not distant or mechanical. It is not cold fate. It is personal and intimately active.

He is not only running the universe; He's holding *you*.

God rules over all things, not just the peaceful moments, but also the painful ones. Like a steady, unseen hand, He guides every detail of our lives, even the ones we do not understand.

Our pain may surprise us, but it never surprises Him. And He never wastes it. He repurposes it with wisdom and love.

God is not scrambling behind the scenes to fix what's gone wrong. He is already bringing beauty from the ashes and purpose from the pain.

Still, when the diagnosis comes... when the loved one

suffers… when the prayers seem to go unanswered… it can feel like the opposite. We wonder: *Is God even here? Is He still in control? Is He still good?*

This is where we need to remember that God's sovereignty is not like the detached power of an earthly ruler. It flows from the heart of a Father who sees, who knows, and cares, and who is very near.

For many, though, even the word *Father* is hard. Perhaps your biological father or father figure left scars instead of safety. Maybe he was harsh, absent, or impossible to please. If that's the image you carry, then the idea of God as Father may not feel comforting.

But God is not like that. He is not distant. He is not demanding. He is not indifferent.

He is the Father who runs toward those who run away from Him. He tends to our wounds, and He prepares feasts when we expect scoldings. He is slow to anger and overflowing with mercy. And even when He allows suffering, it is never to crush us but to rebuild us.

When life falls apart, God doesn't need a backup plan. He is the plan. Even in the pages of life we wish we could rip out, He is writing redemption. Nothing in your story is accidental or wasted.

Scripture provides us with countless reminders of this truth, and one of the clearest is Joseph's story in Genesis. His life was marked by pain. His brothers betrayed him, sold him into slavery, then falsely accused him and left him forgotten in prison. His story reads like tragedy stacked upon tragedy. But then the last chapter turns.

Through it all, God had been working, not erasing Joseph's suffering, but shaping it into something larger. And when Joseph finally stood face to face with the very brothers who had wronged him, his words carried no bitterness, only faith: *"But as for you, ye thought evil against me; but God meant it unto good..."* (Genesis 50:20).

What looked like the end of Joseph's story was actually the beginning of God's preservation for the entire world during a devastating famine. And Scripture doesn't leave us guessing about this. Psalm 105:17 pulls back the curtain on the whole story: God Himself *"sent a man before them"*—Joseph. Long before the famine, long before the betrayal, long before the crisis ever appeared, God had already set the rescue in motion.

This is how God works. He takes what seems ruined and rebuilds it into redemption. He takes betrayal and plants it as the seed of blessing. He turns pain into a platform where His grace is most visible.

I'll be honest, it is not always easy to believe when you're in the middle of suffering. We want the silver lining now. We want the answers now. We want proof that this pain means something. But often, the clarity comes later.

Sometimes, all we can do is trust that God is at work when the heavens feel silent and the lights seem to have gone out. In those moments when the *why* stays unanswered and the ache feels too heavy, we cling to the truth that Scripture repeats again and again.

God is not finished. He is still working. Still redeeming. Still turning tragedies into something beautiful, even in the quiet places of our broken stories.

ORDER OUT OF SUFFERING

One of the hardest challenges about suffering is how messy it feels. Nothing about it is tidy. There are no clean answers, no perfect prayers, and no easy timelines. Suffering feels like chaos, as if life has been flipped upside down and nothing fits anymore.

And yet, in the middle of that turmoil, we discover something unexpected: God is not absent. He is at work.

One of the most comforting truths about His character is that He brings order out of wreckage. He does not promise to prevent suffering, but what He allows, He redeems. He never wastes pain; He transforms it into something that ultimately reflects His glory and works toward our good.

Just look at the life of Daniel, whose story demonstrates that God's faithfulness does not vanish in hardship, it shines brightest there. As a teenager, Daniel was uprooted from his homeland, exiled to Babylon, and thrust into a culture intent on erasing his identity and faith.

Yet he resolved not to defile himself with the king's food offered to idols, a costly choice to remain faithful to the LORD God in a world demanding compromise. And instead of being harmed, he was blessed. God gave him wisdom, favor, and influence. If we could step into that moment, we would see that God was already weaving redemption into the place that seemed most hostile.

Daniel had every reason to give up. Every reason to doubt. But he clung to God. He prayed when prayer was forbidden. He stayed faithful to God when everyone else bowed to idolatry. Decades later, that same faith would lead him into the lion's den. The lions were not merely a punishment; they were meant to be a tomb. But God was not done. He shut the mouths of the lions, and Daniel walked out untouched. What was meant to destroy him became one of the most powerful testimonies of God's deliverance, where chaos gave way to divine order.

This is who God is.

Again and again, the Bible does not show us a God who avoids troubles, but a God who steps into them with His people and brings them through. These are not merely ancient tales; they are reminders for us. No matter how insurmountable our own circumstances may seem, God is still sovereign. Nothing is wasted. In His hands, pain becomes testimony, despair becomes hope, and trials become triumph.

But to see that clearly, we may need to reframe how we think about God's role in our suffering. He is not a bodyguard shielding us from every blow. He is a Master Craftsman. A Restorer of ruins. He gathers the shattered fragments of our lives and fits them into a design far more intricate and precious than we could ever dream.

EMBRACING THE JOURNEY

Maybe you're thinking, *That all sounds nice, but you don't know my story. You don't know what I've been through. No good God would allow what happened to me.*

And you're right, I do not know your story. But I want you to know that I hear you. Truly, I do.

Suffering is not a theory to me. I've lived it. I've endured physical pain that brought me to the edge and emotional wounds that left me speechless. I have prayed prayers through tears, some angry, some desperate, and some barely more than a whisper: *Are You even listening, Lord?*

But I have learned through those seasons that you do not need to have all the answers. It is alright to grieve. It is okay to wrestle with questions. It is even okay to feel like you are falling apart. And what I cling to when everything else gives way is that God is faithful. God is good. And He does not abandon us, even when the road is unbearably dark.

There is a plan. Not only to help you survive, but to redeem every fragment of your story. To restore what was stolen. To heal what was shattered. To write a new chapter when you thought the book was closed. That plan took its greatest step forward the moment Jesus walked out of the grave. His death paid the cost of sin, but His resurrection broke the power of death itself. And from that morning onward, the restoration of all things began, including you.

Yes, the pain we carry here can feel crushing at times. It can feel endless. But it is not forever. It is not the end.

God knows how weary our hearts can grow, so He gave us a glimpse of what's waiting for us in the closing pages of the Bible. In Revelation, He paints a picture of Heaven so vivid you can almost feel the warmth of His hand brushing the tears from your face. A day is coming when death will be gone forever, sorrow will be a fading memory, and every burden you carry now will finally fall away.

That day is real. That day is coming.

But until it arrives, we live in the tension of the *now and not yet*.

We live in the ache and the anticipation.

When answers do not come, and the *why* never gets resolved, when we cannot see what He's doing, God is still at work. He is refining you, strengthening you, and preparing you for what lies ahead. In Christ, suffering does not write the last line. Redemption does.

So, take heart. You do not walk this road by yourself.

And because of that, let's walk it together. With faith, with honesty, and with the quiet confidence that God is not finished yet. He has good plans for you, even here and now, in the midst of pain.

4

LESSONS FROM THE WOUNDED

Sometimes I catch myself wondering what it would have been like to live in a world untouched by suffering. A world without violence, without fear, and without the ache of long goodbyes. Just peace. Just joy. Just God, walking with us in the cool of the day.

From the very moment suffering entered the story with Adam and Eve, God began teaching His people how to live within it by enduring it *with* Him. Centuries later, the desert became a classroom in dependence. Exile stirred up longing for a home beyond this world. Personal loss brought forth deeper trust in His presence. Again and again, He proved that pain in His hands was never wasted; it held purpose.

This changes how I see my own struggles. Suffering is not punishment for every wrong turn, nor is it evidence of abandonment. Often, it is preparation. God uses what hurts to draw us closer, to refine our faith, and to remind us that this broken world is not our forever home. Trials do not exist to destroy us; they are shaping us for greater faith, for deeper joy, and the hope of that day when He wipes away every tear.

So, when I open the Bible and read these ancient stories, I do not only see history, I see hope. The godliest men, women, and even children did not escape trials; they endured unimaginable loss. Through their examples—such as Job, the psalmists, Jeremiah, the Israelites, Paul, and even a nameless servant girl—we are reminded that the same God who carried His people then is faithful still.

Suffering is never easy. It confronts us where we are most vulnerable. But if we let these stories speak, they will show us that God has always been faithful. And to see that faithfulness more clearly, we begin with the story of one man whose name has become synonymous with endurance. If anyone's life captures the collision of suffering and faith, it is Job.

His story reveals what it looks like to walk through unimaginable loss and discover that God is enough to sustain the soul.

JOB:
TRUST IN THE FURNACE OF LOSS

Have you ever had a season where life felt secure, stable even, and then, almost overnight, everything fell apart? One moment you're standing in the sunshine, and the next, you are staring at the wreckage in the dark, wondering how it could crumble so quickly.

That's exactly what happened to a man named Job some 4,000 years ago. He wasn't playing games with his faith. He genuinely loved God, and it showed. People in his community respected him. His land was thriving. His home was filled with laughter. His children were healthy and strong. His life was wrapped in peace.

And then, without warning, he lost everything. Raiders swept in and stole his herds. A fire from heaven consumed his sheep and the servants tending them. And then came the shattering blow: a violent wind struck the house where his children had gathered, and in one terrible instant, the roof collapsed. All of them were dead.

And before the grief could even settle, Job's own health failed. Painful sores covered his skin, and the man who once stood tall and respected now sat in ashes, scraping his wounds with broken pottery.

What I find remarkable about Job's story is its honesty. This is a testimony of a real man crushed by unimaginable grief. And in his anguish, Job didn't pretend everything was fine. He cursed the day of his birth. He poured out raw questions to God, jagged words that cut to the heart of suffering. Yet he brought all of it—his grief, his confusion, even his accusations—to the very One who allowed his suffering. At one point, Job uttered, *"I cry unto thee, and thou dost not hear me..."* (Job 30:20–23). If Job felt unheard, then we should not be surprised when that same ache finds its way into our own hearts.

That tells me that faith isn't pretending you are fine when you are not. Faith is dragging your brokenness to God because, deep down, you know He's the only One who can do something with it, even when you feel unheard and unseen. If you are angry at God, bring that anger to Him. Nowhere in the Bible does God condemn those who pour out their darkest emotions before Him. He is not threatened by honest cries.

That's why Job's story grips me so deeply; it is so real. I've had seasons where one loss hit after the next before I even had time to catch my breath. Maybe you've had them too. That is what makes

Job's testimony so powerful: he did not walk away from the LORD. He wept. He wrestled. He poured out his doubts and frustrations without holding back. And in the middle of it all, he uttered a line that still stops me every time I read it: *"Though he slay me, yet will I trust in him"* (Job 13:15).

It's easy to trust when life feels secure, when prayers are answered, and blessings are piling up. But what about when everything is gone? When Heaven feels silent and grief moves in like a hostile guest? Job shows us that trust doesn't always look like an assured smile or unshakable confidence. Sometimes it looks like scraping your skin with a shard of pottery and whispering through tears, "I still believe."

His faith was not perfect. It was bruised and trembling, but it was alive. No one handles suffering perfectly, and Job proves that imperfect faith is still real faith. And in that wilderness of sorrow, a trust not built on blessings but on God began to take root.

That's the beauty of Job's story. Even while the wounds were still fresh and the questions unanswered, worship still rose from his lips. And though God eventually restored what had been lost, the real treasure wasn't what Job got back in return but who he had become.

Job not only endured the fire. He met God in it. And that gives me hope because if Job's suffering could press him deeper into the heart of God, then ours can too.

THE PSALMISTS:
HONEST CRIES AND HOPE

If Job shows us what it means to wrestle honestly with God in the midst of great loss, the Psalms give us the collective cry of God's people across generations. They are the prayer book of the brokenhearted, the soundtrack of faith amid sorrow.

There have been nights when I've turned to the Psalms with tears still on my face, not looking for easy answers, but simply for a voice that understood. And page after page, I have found it.

The psalmists were not theologians writing from secluded monasteries. They were shepherds, warriors, kings, and exiles. They buried friends, mourned betrayals, and faced the loneliness of caves and watchtowers. Their prayers rose from the trenches of life: fields of battle, prison cells, and tear-soaked beds. The psalmists wrote repeatedly of the ways in which they felt God had afflicted their souls. And when they spoke to God, they did not hold anything back.

Some psalms soar with praise. Others tremble with despair. Together, they paint the full spectrum of what it means to walk with God in a broken world.

One of the most haunting psalms is Psalm 88. It doesn't end with hope as most prayers; the writer pours out his anguish in waves: *"I am counted with them that go down into the pit: I am as a man that hath no strength... Thou hast laid me in the lowest pit, in darkness, in the deeps... Mine eye mourneth by reason of affliction: LORD, I have called daily upon thee, I have stretched out my hands unto thee."* But he doesn't stop at lamenting; he dares to ask the hardest questions: *"LORD, why castest thou off my soul? why hidest thou thy face from me?"* And then he closes with a cry that pierces the heart: *"Lover and friend hast thou put far from me, and mine acquaintance into darkness."*

Reading this psalm can feel like stepping into a dark cave with no light. At first, it unsettles us. Should such despair even be part of God's Word? But then we see the gift hidden in its honesty. God is not afraid of our rawest pleas. He does not reject the prayers that rise from the pit, the sleepless nights, and the grief refuses to loosen its grip. Instead, He welcomes them, holds them, and meets us there.

When I read the psalms, I do not just hear the cries of ancient poets. I hear permission to bring God my own questions, my own frustration, and my own sleepless-night prayers. If God left Psalm 88 in His Word, it means my darkest nights do not disqualify me from His presence. My despair does not drive Him away. On the contrary, He invites me to bring to Him every tear, doubt, and question.

But the Psalms also remind us that grief and hope can live side by side. While some prayers linger in lament, many lift our eyes to the God who binds up the brokenhearted. One of my favorites, Psalm 147:3 says it simply yet profoundly: *"He healeth the broken in heart, and bindeth up their wounds."* I cannot count how many times I've needed that verse to remind me of God's steady nearness when my soul was aching.

That's the beauty of the Psalms. They do not demand we hide our sorrow, nor do they leave us stranded in it. They teach us that faith is not the absence of tears but the decision to bring those tears to God.

That is why, even now, I keep turning to them when my heart is heavy. Because every time I do, I discover again that the same God who met the psalmists in their anguish still meets me in mine.

JEREMIAH:
THE WEEPING PROPHET

If Job shows us suffering in a personal season of life, and the Psalms give us language for shared anguish, then Jeremiah shows us what it is like to carry a heavy heart over an entire lifetime. Commonly known as "the weeping prophet," Jeremiah experienced rejection, misunderstanding, and deep sorrow: hardships that anyone who has carried a burden can recognize. Even as a young man, God called him to stand for the truth, and from that moment, he faced challenges far beyond what he expected.

I sometimes picture him as a young man, still unsure of himself, when God's voice broke into his life with a call that would change everything. Perhaps at first, he thought honor and respect would come with speaking for God. Maybe he imagined his words would inspire people to listen. But instead of applause, he met hostility. He did not stand in a comfortable pulpit with friendly faces nodding *Amen*. He stood before a nation that refused to hear, and most people despised him for it. Friends turned away. Leaders mocked him. And at one point, they even threw him into a muddy cistern and left him there to die.

If you've ever felt abandoned, Jeremiah knew that grief better than most. And yet he kept going.

I try to imagine what it must have been like for him, watching neighbors and perhaps even family, rush headlong into destruction, knowing his words would change nothing. He still loved them. He still showed up. And every time he did, he walked away with another wound because of his faithfulness.

What grips me most is that his tears were not just for himself. They were for his people. He saw what was coming, begged them to turn back, and when they did not, he wept. And he kept on speaking anyway. If I'm honest, I do not know if I could have done that. Could I keep loving people who treated me like an enemy? Could you?

Jeremiah endured, not because he was fearless but because he was faithful. His strength came from knowing the LORD stood with him, even when it didn't feel that way. His pain was not punishment for wandering from God; it was the cost of walking with Him. That is not an easy truth to swallow, but it is one we need. Some of the deepest wounds in life do not come from rebellion; they come from doing what is right. From doing exactly what God asked of you… and paying for it in tears.

So, if you have ever wondered, *Did I do something wrong? Did God leave me?*—Jeremiah's life answers with a quiet but steady no. You are not abandoned. Sometimes God calls us into hard places. He may allow us to feel like we are standing alone for a season, but He *never* leaves us there by ourselves.

Maybe that's the miracle. Not that God always delivers us quickly, but that He stays with us as long as the road requires. Jeremiah's story reminds us that even when the crowd turns away, God does not. And if you have His presence, you truly have enough to keep walking, speaking, and loving… even through the tears.

THE ISRAELITES: FAITH TESTED IN THE WILDERNESS

Have you ever had God come through for you in a way you couldn't possibly miss, and then only a short time later found yourself doubting Him all over again? I wish I could say I have never done that, but I have. It is downright embarrassing how quickly today's fear can swallow yesterday's faith.

When I read about the Israelites, I realize we are not so different from them after all. Few stories capture the tension between God's faithfulness and human weakness as vividly as Israel's journey from Egypt to the Promised Land.

When God delivered His people from slavery, it was nothing short of miraculous. They had just walked out of Egypt after centuries of slavery. They had seen the Nile turn to blood, the plagues fall, and Pharaoh bow his head. They felt the rush of hope as God led them out with the spoils of Egypt. You'd think trust would have come easily after that.

But it did not take long for fear to rise again.

Just days later, the sound of chariots thundered behind them. Pharaoh had changed his mind about letting the Israelites leave, and dust clouds marked the army closing in. Panic swept through the people, and they lashed out at Moses: *"Because there were no graves in Egypt, hast thou taken us away to die in the wilderness?"* (Exodus 14:11).

When I read that, I want to shake my head: *Really? After all God just did?* But then I remember my own heart, and I see myself in them, those low moments in my life when I forget yesterday's miracles in the face of today's challenges, when my memory fails me concerning God's faithfulness.

So, how did the LORD respond to their panic? He did not rebuke them. He made a way. He split the sea, pulled back the waters, and walked them through on dry ground.

But even that miracle did not steel their trust for long.

Soon hunger set in, and instead of calling out in faith, they grumbled again: *"Would to God we had died... for ye have brought us forth into this wilderness, to kill this whole assembly with hunger."* (Exodus 16:3). A pattern began to repeat: God provided. The people complained. He showed mercy. They forgot.

For two years, God proved Himself faithful again and again. And then they reached the border of the Promised Land, the place God had been leading them all along. All they had to do was trust Him one more time and cross over. But fear convinced them they were already defeated. They cried out: *"Would God that we had died in the land of Egypt!"* (Numbers 14:2).

That was the moment everything shifted. God's patience is long, but it is not endless. He told Moses He would start over, but in mercy, He spared them when Moses and Aaron interceded. And so they wandered for the next thirty-eight years, until every unbelieving heart was buried in the sand.

It's a sobering story. What broke God's heart was their refusal to believe He cared. He had proven Himself faithful again and again, and still they turned back to fear. And yet, even in the middle of judgment, there was grace. Even in wandering, there was hope. God didn't walk away. He still provided manna. He still guided with fire and cloud. He still longed for their trust.

That has not changed. If we look closely, we can see it was always that way. Even in the hardest parts of the Old Testament—judgment, wandering, loss—hope still flickered. There was always a heartbeat of grace pulsing beneath the story: a God who does not change. A God who still longs for our trust, still provides for our needs, and yes, still grieves when we run to other sources for comfort instead of Him.

UNNAMED SERVANT GIRL

There is a little story, only a few lines long, tucked away in 2 Kings that is easy to miss, but every time I read it, it lingers with me. It is about a nameless young Israelite girl whose life was turned upside down in a single moment. One day, she was home with her family. Next, a Syrian raid tore everything away. She was dragged off captive to a foreign land, surrounded by strangers speaking a language she didn't know. She did not know if her parents were alive. She did not know if she'd ever see her home again. She was just… a girl.

Can you imagine the terror? The confusion? The nights she must have cried into her blanket in those first weeks? I wonder if she prayed for rescue, and if she ever wondered whether God was even listening? Most of us might expect her story to fade into bitterness, and who could blame her? She had not done anything to deserve what happened. But that is not how her story ends.

Instead of letting sorrow harden her heart, this girl let faith rise. One day, she overheard that Naaman, the commander of the army that had stolen her, had leprosy. Instead of thinking, *Good, now he'll suffer like I have,* she did something extraordinary. She spoke up. She told his wife about a prophet in Israel, a man of God who could heal him.

That still stuns me. Where did that kind of heart, that kind of mercy, come from? She was just a nameless servant girl in the household of her captors. And yet she still believed God was who He said He is. That belief kept her tender, even in her loss. And in her grief, she became the unlikely messenger who pointed Naaman to the only God who could heal him.

Her story makes me think: if she could speak faith in the middle of her loss, what might God be asking me to do in mine? Her life proves that circumstances do not get the final say in how brightly we shine. She was far from home, stripped of freedom, surrounded by people who did not share her faith, and still, God's light reached through her. That is not just her story; it is ours too. God can use us in the most unexpected places: hospital rooms, courtrooms, prison cells, and grief-soaked kitchens. When we let Him, our lives can bring hope into someone else's darkness.

It amazes that God did not wait to use her until she was free or until her life made sense again. He used her right where she was: in captivity, in loss, in the middle of a story she never asked for. God's light does not wait for perfect conditions. It shines even when we feel small, unseen, and far from where we want to be.

PAUL:
STRENGTH IN WEAKNESS

From the obscurity of the servant girl, we now turn to one of the most well-known figures in the New Testament, the Apostle Paul. His life offers perhaps the clearest New Testament example of what it means to discover that God's grace is enough in the midst of suffering.

When I think of Paul, it's easy to picture the bold preacher, the missionary who planted churches, wrote letters, and stood before rulers without flinching. But if we actually read Scripture, we see that his story is not a tale of unshakable strength. It is the story of a man who was broken, battered, and often at the end of himself. Yet, somehow, he kept going.

Paul knew suffering well. He had been beaten many times, betrayed, shipwrecked three times, and locked behind prison walls frequently. But beyond the physical pain and public trials, each hardship carried its own deeper cost: long stretches of separation from family, friends, and the communities he loved. Those he longed to embrace were often out of reach, leaving him to endure hardship and profound solitude.

On top of all that, he carried something far more personal, which he described as a *"thorn in the flesh."* We do not know exactly what it was, but whatever it may have been, it never let him forget his limits. He begged God to take it away. I can almost picture him praying those prayers with all his heart, waiting for relief. But the answer he received was not the one he wanted. God said, *"My grace is sufficient for thee: for my strength is made perfect in weakness"* (2 Corinthians 12:9).

I don't know about you, but at first, that feels almost disappointing. Paul asked for healing, and instead God gave him grace. He wanted the thorn gone, and God let it stay. But in that place of weakness, Paul discovered something he never could have learned otherwise: weakness was not a failure. It was the place where Christ's power rested.

This turns the world's definition of power on its head. We are taught to push harder, prove ourselves, and overcome through force of will. But God invites us to stop striving and lean on His grace instead. When Paul stopped striving for escape and began yielding to grace, something changed. Weakness became a doorway. Dependence became strength. His limitation became the place where Christ's power was most visible. It was not that grace replaced the thorn; it outshone it. And Paul discovered what we all must: the end of ourselves is often the place where God begins His deepest work.

So, when you come to the end of yourself, like Paul once did, you are standing at the beginning of grace. Grace is not fragile; it is the strength that lifts you when yours is gone and carries you when you cannot stand. That's why Paul could write, almost shockingly, *"Most gladly therefore will I rather glory in my infirmities, that the power of Christ may rest upon me... for when I am weak, then am I strong"* (vs. 10).

He was not pretending pain was desirable. He was not shrugging it off. He was saying, "This is where I've met God most deeply. In the vulnerable places I wish were different."

And it makes me wonder how many of us spend our lives trying to hide weakness, when it might actually be the stage where God desires His strength to shine.

I have often wondered how Paul kept going when so much seemed stacked against him. It all comes down to what he valued most. For Paul, the goal of life wasn't comfort or ease; it was Christ Himself. That's why, even in the midst of suffering, he was never sidelined from usefulness. Instead, suffering became the place where Christ's power was most visible. Sitting in a prison cell, he could write, *"...for I have learned, in whatsoever state I am, therewith to be content"*. And facing uncertainty, he could still say, *"For to me to live is Christ, and to die is gain"* (Philippians 4:11 & 1:21).

That kind of courage comes from leaning into grace. Paul had already surrendered everything, and in that place, he discovered the astonishing truth that Christ's grace truly is enough, even when nothing else is. He didn't grit his teeth and tolerate weakness; he embraced it with peace. In a world that hides weakness, Paul put his on display because it was there that Christ's strength was revealed.

So, what if we began to see suffering that way? What if, instead of scrambling to escape it, we let it become the place where

God's grace does its deepest work?

I find this encouraging because, like Paul, I have prayed for God to take away my discomfort. Sometimes He has. Other times, He has not. But when He has not, I have found the same truth Paul did: Christ meets us in weakness, and His strength carries us when our own has run out.

So whatever your "thorn" may be: illness, loss, disappointment, limitation—don't believe the lie that God cannot use you until it's gone. Paul's story tells us the opposite. God's grace shows up in the place you wish were different. His reminder to Paul is His assurance to us as well: *"My grace is sufficient for thee."* Even in the thorn, even in the trial, God's grace is enough.

JESUS CHRIST:
THE MAN OF SORROWS

He who understands suffering best is Jesus Christ. The Prophet Isaiah describes the Messiah as the One who was *"oppressed and afflicted"* and the One who *"hath borne our griefs, and carried our sorrows"* (Isaiah 53). Every page of His life bears the mark of pain, rejection, and sorrow. And unlike all the earlier examples taken together, He willingly stepped into it.

Think of how His story begins. The eternal Son of God, who lived in glory with the Father, took on human flesh. He did not enter a palace, wrapped in silk and guarded by servants; He entered through the labor pains of a poor teenage girl. His first cradle was not a carved crib but an animal's feeding trough. The Lord of all creation began His earthly life in a stable, with the stench of livestock in His nostrils.

Before He was even old enough to speak, His parents fled to Egypt as refugees, escaping Herod's soldiers who were slaughtering infants in search of Him. He entered our world marked by danger, poverty, and rejection.

As He grew, misunderstanding and ridicule followed Him. Nazareth was an obscure, overlooked village with no honor, and He bore its stigma. Neighbors sneered: "Isn't this the carpenter's son?" "We know His brothers. Who does He think He is?" Even His own family doubted Him, mocking His mission. As John tells us plainly: *"He came unto his own, and his own received him not"* (John 1:11).

At the start of His ministry, Jesus drew a large crowd to a hillside. Word had spread about Him, and people came with all kinds of hopes and ideas. Some may have expected a political revolution, a leader rising to challenge Rome. But what they heard was a different kind of revolution, one that would turn their understanding of blessing and suffering upside down.

The crowd leaned in, waiting for words that might change everything. Then Jesus said: *"Blessed are they which are persecuted for righteousness' sake...Blessed are ye, when men shall revile you, and persecute you, and shall say all manner of evil against you falsely...Rejoice"* (Matthew 5:10-12).

I can almost imagine the crowd glancing at each other in disbelief. *Rejoice? In persecution?* It didn't make sense. And yet He meant it. He was telling them, 'Your suffering is not wasted.' You are walking the same road as the prophets before you, and the same road I am walking with you now.

Throughout His ministry, the religious leaders who should have welcomed the Messiah instead schemed to trap Him, calling Him demon-possessed, a blasphemer, a drunkard, and a friend of sinners. Even the crowds who marveled at His miracles later shouted for His crucifixion. Like so many of us, He experienced the sting of being misjudged and rejected by those He longed to love, and He endured it.

His ministry was marked by endless demands. People pressed in on Him from dawn to dusk, desperate for healing, deliverance, food, and hope. He touched the untouchable, ate with outcasts, lifted the broken-hearted. But each miracle and every teaching came at the cost of His own weariness. So often the Gospels tell us He withdrew to secluded places to pray. Can you imagine the exhaustion of carrying the weight of the world's needs on your shoulders, day after day? He knows what it is to be poured out until nothing is left.

The world celebrates the admired, powerful, and the honored. But Jesus looked at the rejected, the mistreated, the misunderstood, and declared that *they* are the ones closest to Heaven. Their pain was not meaningless. It drew them into fellowship with Him.

Observing Jesus endure what no one should bear, I realize that suffering can be borne with dignity, even when relief does not come. Sometimes God answers with ease, sometimes with presence, and in His case, presence transforms suffering into salvation. What once felt unbearable is given a new name; He calls it "blessed," treats it with honor, and most of all, stays with us, never leaving us alone in the midst of it.

In Jesus, suffering itself was defeated. The stone rolled away. He rose again. Death could not hold Him. The One acquainted with grief now stood victorious, His wounds still visible, transformed from signs of defeat into trophies of redemption. Through His death and resurrection, He broke the power of sin, death, and despair. He turned the world's darkest hour into Heaven's greatest victory.

This is why the *man of sorrows* can sit with you in your tears and also lift you in your hope. If you feel abandoned, He knows the ache of loneliness. If you feel crushed, He knows the burden of despair. If you feel forsaken, He has walked that road Himself. Yet He did not remain in sorrow; He overcame it. That is why our suffering is never endured alone. Jesus is not a distant observer of our pain; He is present in it, sharing every struggle.

The Book of Hebrews reminds us that we have a High Priest who sympathizes with our weaknesses, for He was tempted in every way, just as we are, yet without sin. And He does not simply offer words of comfort; He offers the witness of His scars—living proof that our pain is never wasted.

Our pain, when united with His, is never meaningless. The cross shows us that agony can hold redemption and that grief can bear fruit. Paul said he longed to *"know Christ... and the fellowship of his sufferings"* (Philippians 3:10). To share in His suffering is to walk the same road that leads to resurrection glory.

Jesus' story changes the way we view our own. We may not understand every "why," but we know "Who". We know the One who entered into sorrow, conquered it, and now walks with us through it. We know the One who promises that one day every tear will be wiped away, because He has already secured the victory.

This is the promise of the *man of sorrows*: that no grief is wasted, no wound ignored, and no heart abandoned. He knows the way through the dark. And because He has already triumphed, we can trust that one day, every tear will be wiped away, and love, not sorrow, will have the final word.

A HOLY INVITATION

Pain has a way of making itself known. It is not something we can push to the side, no matter how we try. I know because I've tried.

I think back to nights at three in the morning when back spasms made even breathing feel like a battle. The room was silent except for the hum of a fan. I lay there in the dark, aching with pain and feeling isolated with no one to help. That kind of pain presses in and lingers. And if you are not careful, it starts hissing its lies.

But even there, I began to notice something. Suffering brings with it an invitation to draw closer to the One who knows suffering better than anyone else. It is not a road I would have chosen, but unexpectedly, it has led me into corners of God's heart I might never have seen otherwise. In its peculiar way, suffering becomes a lifeline within the dark, pulling me, step by step, closer to Christ.

Jesus never minimized what life would be like. He spoke with striking honesty, like a faithful friend looking you in the eye: *"These things I have spoken unto you, that in me ye might have peace. In the world ye shall have tribulation: but be of good cheer; I have overcome the world"* (John 16:33).

He does not hide the hardship; He names it. And He does not stop there. He anchors us in peace in Him. The pain is real, yes—but so is the victory. And His words strike at the roots of everything that breaks us: sin and death.

That is why Jesus' words still breathe life: *"If any man thirst, let him come unto me, and drink"* (John 7:37). He does not call us to deny our need or pretend we are strong. He speaks to thirst, to the ache that pain creates. He invites us to come as we are, empty and weary, and receive what only He can give. And in drawing near to Him, something begins to change within us.

If you look back at Job in the ashes, Jeremiah in tears, the unnamed servant girl in captivity, the Israelites in the wilderness, the psalmists crying out in the dark, Paul with his thorn, and Jesus on the cross, they are all telling us the same message: suffering is not the end. It can be the beginning of something beautiful. Suffering has a way of transforming us, and even those who watch us. Some of the most unforgettable testimonies are written in hospital rooms, prison cells, and grief-soaked bedrooms, places we never would have chosen.

So I hold on to the certainty that God is good, even when life is not. He is working, even when I cannot see it. He is enough, even when I feel empty. Suffering may press us down, but it presses us deeper into Him.

When the night feels unbearably long, I remember that morning is still coming. And that morning's name is Jesus Christ.

5

WHEN GOD FEELS SILENT

It happened a few years ago. An episode that pushed my body, faith, and sanity to the edge. The back pain I inherited from my mother grew into a monster far beyond discomfort. One particular flare-up took everything to a new level: my personal "Lion's Den" moment. Pain shot through my lower back, hips, and legs like fiery knives, tearing me apart. I could not stand, walk, or work. I was confined to bed for months, broken in every way a man can be. And the silence from God? It was unbearable.

I remember lying sprawled across the floor in whatever crooked position I could manage, tears streaming down my face, pleading, "God, where are You?" Over and over, I begged Him to speak, to show up, to do something. But instead of comfort or clarity, all I met was silence. No answers. No voice. Just the walls of my home pressing in, and the grief in my soul growing louder than the ache in my body.

And in that silence, the questions I had for God grew sharper:

Was I being punished? Had I done something wrong? Was He angry with me?

When Heaven feels quiet, the mind starts to wander, and the heart becomes a battlefield all its own. The devil does not waste moments like these. He circles like a vulture, waiting for anything that looks like weakness. "God has abandoned you," he hisses. "You're not worth His time." And when your body is wrecked and your spirit drained, those lies sound an awful lot like truth.

The silence was deafening. It felt like abandonment. But it did not end there. Somewhere in that stillness, something began to stir within me. Slowly, quietly, God was showing me that His silence had more to say than I realized.

THE MEANING OF SILENCE

I have come to realize in the wilderness of suffering that what feels like divine silence is not always what it seems. Somewhere in the silence, right in the middle of my agony, I began to understand that God was not ignoring me. He was not angry. He had not gone anywhere. He was inviting me to trust Him in a way I never had before. Slowly, I began to see that His silence was not rejection; it was refining. He was not absent; His nearness was simply soft and quiet. He was working deep within me in ways I could not recognize at the time. He was shaping me through what I had mistaken for silence.

I remember softly singing the lines of an old hymn as I lay on the floor, barely able to move...

Be still, my soul:
the Lord is on thy side;
bear patiently the cross of grief or pain.

Those words were more than lyrics to me; they were survival. They were the rope I clung to when everything else felt like it was slipping away. And God began softening my heart.

I soon came to realize that God never left me. He was there the whole time, sitting with me, weeping with me, and holding me even when I could not feel Him. Little by little, I learned to trust Him again, not because the pain stopped, but because His goodness did not.

THE SPACE TO FEEL

Why, in my pain, was I so quick to think that God had abandoned me? What I eventually realized was that I didn't just want comfort. I wanted control. I wanted to move again. Serve again. Do again. My life had a rhythm, a plan, a purpose. And pain shattered all of it. I had dreams and ambitions. Goals. Ministry I was building. Good things. And yet God allowed it all to grind to a halt. I was not just in pain; I was offended.

I remember muttering through clenched teeth, "Why would You let this happen to me? Don't You see what I'm trying to do for You?"

And in that place, I learned that sometimes God's silence is the only thing strong enough to stop us from shouting over Him. Just like a child throwing a tantrum, we need space to feel, to process, and to unravel a little. And God, in His mercy, gives us that space. He is not intimidated by our emotions. He does not shame us for falling apart. He lets us feel it all, and then, in time, He gently invites us back to trust.

When the fury burns out, when the tears finally run dry, and you lift your head with swollen eyes and a heart cracked wide open, you begin to hear Him again, because the noise inside you has finally quieted enough to listen.

SEEING AND REPENTING OF SIN

Suffering reveals a lot. When everything else was stripped away, what I saw staring back at me was… me. And honestly, it wasn't very pretty. Flat on the floor, God started showing me attitudes within me that I had never seen before.

For years, I had silently judged others. I noticed their flaws, inconsistencies, and failures, harboring little verdicts against them in my heart. I may not have said it out loud, but my thoughts could be incredibly critical. I assumed I knew the story behind someone's struggle. I thought I could size them up spiritually. But in my suffering, that pride cracked wide open.

Over time, I could feel the battles people were fighting beneath the surface. I understood their invisible agony because I was living it. And it changed me. The longer I sat in pain, the softer my heart became. It wasn't that I had suddenly grown more compassionate, but that desperation forced me to see people differently. Who was I to judge someone else's walk when I could not even crawl through mine?

That season, as physically tormenting as it was, became spiritual surgery. God was cutting deeper than I realized, removing attitudes in me that did not reflect Christ. He was cleansing my soul. Looking back, I can see sins that had been hiding in me all along, tendencies I never noticed when life was undisturbed. But suffering brought them to the surface. And in the silence, I realized God was doing the slow, careful work of a Master Surgeon.

It hurt. It broke me. But I'll tell you the truth: I wouldn't trade it now because on the other side of it, I see Jesus more clearly, and I see myself more honestly.

BIBLICAL ENCOURAGEMENT IN THE SILENCE

When I turn to the Bible, I do not just read stories of people who heard God loud and clear. I notice people who walked through His silence and came out changed.

I think of Hagar, a servant girl caught in the middle of a desperate plan. Sarai gave her to Abram to bear a child, but when jealousy rose, Hagar was cast aside. She fled into the wilderness, pregnant, alone, and unseen. For a time, there was no voice from Heaven. Just silence. But in that wilderness, when she had nowhere left to run, God drew near and asked a question: *"Hagar, whence camest thou? and whither wilt thou go?"* (Genesis 16:8). In that moment, she realized she had never been invisible to Him. He had heard her affliction.

And Hagar, the one everyone else had forgotten, became the first person in Scripture to call God: *El Roi*, the God who sees me (vs. 13). She discovered that even when Heaven felt quiet, His eyes had never left her.

I also think of Hannah, whose story always touches me. Year after year, she longed for a child, and for so long, her prayers seemed to fall into silence. As if her grief was not heavy enough, the other woman in her home only deepened the ache in her heart. And in the temple, where she hoped to find comfort, she was misunderstood by the priest and accused of being drunk. The loneliness of that moment is almost unimaginable. Yet, Hannah kept praying, through the tears, through the silence, through the ache that would not lift. When God moved at last, His answer was more than the gift of a child; it was an invitation for Hannah to trust Him so deeply that she could place that child back into His hands without worry.

And of course, I cannot overlook Jesus. In Gethsemane, under the crushing weight of what was coming, He pleaded with the Father: "If there's any other way..." But Heaven stayed silent. And Jesus chose to drink the cup. That silence was not absence but the path to redemption.

WHEN SIN CREATES SILENCE

There have been times when I have sat in the quiet and wondered why God felt so far away. Looking back, I realize it was not that He had turned His back on me. It was that I had allowed unresolved matters pile up in my own heart.

Maybe you've felt it too, slowly building, bitterness you cannot quite release. Unforgiveness you tuck away but keep close. Pride that hints you don't really need to bend to God's will. It does not take much before all of it starts clogging the line between you and the Father.

I have learned something hard but freeing: God's silence can be an invitation to let Him search our hearts and ask, "Lord, is there something I'm holding onto that's keeping me from hearing You?" God's silence can certainly test our trust in Him. And when it does, we face a defining choice: to lean on what we feel or to rest in what we know to be true of His character: that He is good, faithful, and near.

One bit of hope we can hold onto in the face of what we perceive as God's silence is this: He is not ignoring us. He is waiting and longing for us to crack open the door of our hearts so He can rush in with healing. And that door only swings open on the hinge of surrender.

FINDING PEACE IN THE QUIET

If I could go back and sit beside that younger version of myself, curled up in pain, crying out into what felt like an empty room, I would take his hand and say: You are not alone, not even for a single moment.

Looking back now, I can see that the deepest growing I've ever done happened during long stretches of what I thought was silence. Over time, I began to realize that silence can be God's way of pulling us closer, of healing places in us we did not even know were broken. In other words, the silence is not rejection, it is love. And in that quiet, you are being pursued and purposed. God uses our pain and His silence to prepare us, refine us, and remind us that our faith is not built on how loudly He speaks but on how deeply we trust Him.

And one day, when the silence lifts (and it will), you will look back and realize that God was not absent. He was closer than ever.

6

DISCOVERING GOD'S PRESENCE

There is a kind of suffering that does more than hurt the body. There's a more insidious form of pain that drains the vibrance out of life and leaves you struggling to breathe, wondering how you will face another day.

It might come through the death of someone dear, where their absence follows you into every quiet room. It might arrive through betrayal, when a trusted friend wounds you so deeply that trust itself feels foreign. Or it may take the form of long, restless nights when grief presses so heavily on your chest that words for prayer are hard to come by.

In those moments, the silence itself feels crushing, and the deepest questions arise: *Where is God in all this? Is God even a part of my life anymore?*

I have asked those same questions myself during some of my darkest days. In those moments, I, too, wondered whether God had turned His face away from me.

If you have cried the same words aloud or felt them simmering inside, you are standing in a long line of faithful hearts. You are definitely not weak. You are not without faith. And you are certainly not someone whom God has turned His back on. You are simply human, and someone in need of love, support, and care.

Followers of Christ through the centuries have wept the same tears and begged Heaven for a sign of comfort, only to be met with silence. Many have walked into the church house wearing smiles while their hearts felt like an empty tomb.

And yet, we have also seen people we deem "extraordinary Christians" who endure immense suffering with an almost unshakable peace. Their world is collapsing, but somehow they remain steady, convinced that God is near. Watching them, you may have wondered: *How? How can they hold on when I feel like I'm barely standing?*

If you've ever questioned why you can't seem to hold on as they do, you are not failing at faith. Suffering has a way of exposing the tender places in us, those fragile spots we did not even realize were there. It can leave you feeling as though you're slipping, as if faith is something other people carry better than you.

I understand that feeling more than I wish I did. I have walked through seasons when God's silence stung, when prayer felt like it fell back onto my shoulders, when abandonment seemed easier to believe than hope. Pain in those moments confuses, unsettles, and shakes everything you thought you knew.

Sometimes, when confusion clouds everything, I have found it helps to go back to the place where I first knew beyond a shadow of a doubt that God was real. Not to search for answers. Rather, I return to the beginnings of my faith, to reconnect with the God who met me in the earliest days of my journey.

And when I look back on those first steps of walking with God, one heavenly truth endures: *we are never forsaken.* Even when our emotions insist otherwise, God is near, and He cares deeply for you. The ache of isolation, though painfully real, often reveals our human limits more than His presence. His nearness is not measured by what we feel, but by the unchanging truth of who He is.

The Bible is filled with reminders of this assurance. Sometimes the words come gently, as in Psalm 119:151, *"Thou art near, O LORD."* Other times, they come with strong tenderness, like in Zephaniah 3:17: *"The LORD thy God in the midst of thee is mighty; he will save."* These are not merely poetic phrases meant to soothe us. They are promises, anchors for the moments when you feel unseen by God or overlooked by the world. They reassure you that He still sees you… And He will never leave you nor forsake you.

When God feels far, it does not mean He has withdrawn. Often it is His way of drawing us to lean more deeply on what is true rather than what is felt: His faithful love and His unbroken presence (what is true). This does not erase the heaviness of grief (what is felt), but it gives us something solid to hold on to when everything else feels unsteady.

So, if the heaviness of grief, confusion, or fear begins to rise within you, bring it to Christ. You were never meant to carry it by yourself. The One strong enough to carry the cross is strong enough to bear your burdens, too.

CONNECT YOUR PAIN TO CHRIST'S

When pain crashes into our lives, the first cry of our heart is often: "God, make it stop." We beg for relief, plead for rest, and hope the weight will lift. Sometimes God, in His mercy, does calm the storm. But more often, His deepest work is revealed not by removing the struggle but by staying with us through it. In every season of heartache I have faced, God has shown His loving kindness in unexpected and tender ways.

There is a nearness to God that often comes in difficulty and despair. When sorrow refuses to lift and weakness clings to your soul, His presence can become more real than you ever imagined. It may not come in an audible voice, but through His Word, or through gentle reminders carried by friends, family, and even strangers. His grace strengthens you to take one more breath, one more step. God may not erase the pain, but He fills it with Himself. And in that filling, He gives your suffering a purpose: drawing you so close at times, it feels as though you can sense His very heartbeat.

Our suffering transforms most clearly when we connect it to Christ's suffering. He does not stand far off, untouched by human sorrow. He knew betrayal. He felt abandonment. He grieved at gravesides. He sweat drops of blood in a garden. God is not distant from pain.

And if you wonder what God's presence looks like in the midst of suffering, you do not have to search far. Look at Jesus. Look at His pierced hands, His tear-streaked face, His body broken for us. In Him, God's nearness took on flesh and bone. In Him, we are given the wonderful assurance that our suffering is never faced alone.

He is *Emmanuel—God with us.* Not hovering nearby, but dwelling within. Through the Holy Spirit, Christ makes His home in your heart. You do not walk through suffering searching for Him. You carry Him wherever you go.

Let that truth offer sweet relief and rest when the heaviness you feel is unbearable. When your strength falters, let His Word speak into the ache: *"It is good for me to draw near to God..."* (Psalm 73:28). *"Draw nigh to God, and he will draw nigh to you"* (James 4:8). *"God is our refuge and strength, a very present help in trouble"* (Psalm 46:1). These verses do not diminish your suffering. They declare that suffering is not the final word. God is your lifeline, your unwavering supporter, present in every joy, every fear, and every need.

Think about Shadrach, Meshach, and Abednego. They were thrown into the furnace for refusing to bow, and I often wonder if their knees trembled as they stood before the king. Yet in the fire, they were not alone. A fourth figure walked with them. The fire did not consume them, nor did the smell of smoke cling to their clothes. God did not keep them from entering the furnace; He met them there.

Isaiah 43:2 carries that same promise: *"When thou passest through the waters, I will be with thee; and through the rivers, they shall not overflow thee: when thou walkest through the fire, thou shalt not be burned; neither shall the flame kindle upon thee."* Those words are not exaggerations; they are assurances. God does not abandon you to the overwhelming and terrifying trials of life, nor to leave you to fend for yourself through disappointments that press in along the way. He steps into the fire with you and carries you through every step.

So, if you have ever questioned whether God understands your pain, remember this: He bore His own suffering so you would never walk through yours alone. In your most overwhelming moments—

whether grief, loss, or physical agony—you may be closer to Jesus than you realize.

When your suffering is joined with Christ's, it becomes something extraordinary. The pain may remain, but it takes on a new purpose. It becomes a place where He shapes you, strengthens you, and draws you to His heart. And friend, He sees every tear, knows every scar, and promises that your story is nowhere near finished.

PRESENCE IN DEPENDENCE

Some of the most heart-wrenching questions suffering often brings are, "Where *is* God right now? Why can't I feel Him?" Scripture assures us again and again that He is near, yet our hearts often ache with silence. So what is the disconnect?

What I've learned over time is that the problem is not God's absence. It is the barriers we raise between ourselves and His presence, barriers often built from our misguided desire to handle life on our own.

Pain has a way of driving us inward. We unintentionally pull back and shut ourselves off from the very support God placed around us: friends, loved ones, His Word, and His Spirit within us. We slip into survival mode, leaning on self-protection and self-reliance. We think, *if I just work harder... if I just figure this out... if I just stay strong...* Before long, we stop leaning on the One who has already offered to carry what we cannot.

This pattern is not new. In the Garden of Eden, Eve heard the whisper that she couldn't trust God and had to look out for herself. That same deception still tempts us today, convincing us that dependence is weakness and that strength comes only through our own effort. And somehow, we continue to believe that lie.

Yet suffering exposes this struggle. The challenge is not only in bearing the pain but in choosing whether we will retreat into ourselves or collapse into God's care. That kind of surrender can feel frightening and incredibly vulnerable because it requires letting go of control. And if you are like me, letting go does not come easily.

Dependence means trust, the willingness to say, "Lord, I accept what You've placed before me, and I trust You to supply the strength I need." It rarely feels natural. Yet it is often in that very surrender that His presence becomes tangible, and with it, a comfort no human words can fully describe.

I have seen this in my own life. There were seasons when I followed God's leading while carrying heavy burdens of worry about money, work, and personal struggles. I kept praying and serving even when I felt completely worn out. In those moments when life seemed empty and I had nothing left to give, I laid it all before Him. Sometimes hesitantly, often little by little, and that is where His strength met me and carried me through.

If you long to feel His nearness in the midst of suffering, you might begin by asking yourself: *Am I holding something back? Am I still depending on myself instead of God? Am I trusting Him with my finances or only what's left over? Am I giving Him my time in prayer or only the scraps of my energy? Am I looking to His Word each day or just hoping the Sunday sermon carries me through the week?*

Dependence is not weakness. It is the humble confession, "Lord, I cannot do this without You," and the recognition that we were never meant to do so. God's presence does not always arrive with fanfare; more often, it comes quietly, steadying us, holding us upright when we have no strength of our own.

And let me be clear: dependence does not cancel responsibility. God does not call us to throw wisdom aside or gamble our futures away. He is not hiding behind a lottery ticket or waiting in a casino. He meets us in the small, faithful steps of obedience that rarely make sense at first. *That* is where He supplies strength that endures and provision that does not run dry.

So, I return again and again to one simple question: *Is my suffering drawing me deeper into His arms, or driving me further into myself?*

The answer often reveals more than I expect. And in that answer, I begin to see the nearness of God I have been searching for all along. This same closeness with the Great Comforter and Redeemer is available to you as well.

PRACTICE WAITING

Waiting is one of the hardest practices of the Christian life. Few things test our faith more than silence and delay.

We pray. We plead. We pace. We check the time, check our hearts, check the heavens—and still, no response. The silence stretches on, and we begin to wonder if anything is happening at all.

If you are like me, and like most people shaped by the convenience of modern life, waiting feels like wasted time. We live in a world wired for speed. Tap a screen, and dinner shows up at the door. Type a question, and AI spits back a response. We are conditioned to expect results now, faster, cheaper, easier. And when our expectations are not met, we grow restless and frustrated.

We may not voice it, but in our minds, we begin to view God more like an on-demand product delivery service than the Creator who holds our lives in His hands.

But that impatience can be dangerous, even poisonous, for the soul. It tempts us to resist surrender, to despise patience, and to assume that God must operate on our schedule. Yet often, the waiting itself is an act of mercy.

Sometimes the delay is God's way of loosening our grip on every false source of confidence: our abilities, our plans, even the people we depend on more than Him. In the waiting, He draws us to rest our confidence in Him. He breaks down the empty securities we try to cling to and feeds us with something far richer than shortcuts to healing. He loves us too much to let us live on substitutes that cannot sustain us.

Waiting uncovers the idols of comfort and convenience we've built around ourselves. It strips away the illusion that we are managing life on our own. And in that empty space, it invites us into a deeper faith: a slower, steadier trust in the God who sees what we cannot.

Why does He so often choose waiting as the setting for His greatest work? Because waiting forms us. It quiets the noise inside us. It reveals cracks in our foundation that we never noticed. And most of all, it makes room for dependence on Him.

This is why the Scripture speaks of waiting not as a punishment but as a source of strength. *"Wait on the LORD: be of good courage, and he shall strengthen thine heart"* (Psalm 27:14). *"They that wait upon the LORD shall renew their strength"* (Isaiah 40:31). Waiting may feel like wasted time, but it is training your faith. And that faith helps teach you to stand even when your heart is trembling.

David understood this. He wrote, *"I waited patiently for the LORD; and he inclined unto me, and heard my cry"* (Psalm 40:1). Those words came from a man who knew what it meant to be pressed by trouble and wearied by sorrow, yet he remained convinced that God had not abandoned him.

When we lean on and put our confidence in God, His presence changes the very nature of our waiting. Panic gives way to peace. Confusion settles beneath His clarity. Strength begins to seep into broken places that we thought were beyond repair.

Sometimes the waiting is His preparation for what lies ahead. Often, it is His reshaping of our character. And it is always an invitation from God to draw nearer to Him. In these seasons, God not only reveals more profoundly what He can do, but He also reveals who He is.

He is not late. He is not absent. He is near.

When the waiting feels unbearable, His nearness is the anchor. It may not take the ache away, but it gives the ache meaning. Because when the silence finally lifts, we begin to see God has been at work all along, doing more in us during the waiting than we ever could have imagined.

REFLECT ON GOD'S PROMISES

One of the promises of God I have leaned on the most, both in joy and in pain, is simple yet profound: God is near. Not just when the sun is shining or when I feel capable, but also in sorrow, when tears blur my vision and nothing makes sense.

In Psalm 145:18, we are given assurance: *"The LORD is nigh unto all them that call upon him, to all that call upon him truth."* Those words are not poetic filler. They are a declaration from the Creator: I am with you.

Yet if we are honest, our emotions rarely line up with that truth. Suffering has a way of twisting our perception. Sad, scared, and even angry feelings whisper, "You're alone." Doubt creeps in, makes the lie feel real. Before long, we begin living as if our emotions carry more authority than God's promises.

That is why, during seasons of heartache and what feels like silence, I have had to press intentionally into Scripture. When the noise is stripped away, God's Word breaks through with greater clarity. In the quiet, His promises resonate in ways they rarely do when life is crowded with distractions.

The Bible cannot sit on the shelf as an occasional reference; it is meant to be our anchor. We must steady our hearts with it, keeping it close when our thoughts run wild. We must place His words where we can see them daily: on the refrigerator, in the car, on the mirror. We must read them when sleep won't come and speak them aloud when anxiety rises. The Holy Bible is our lifeline—God's gift to guide us, strengthen us, and steady us. And we need to cling to it daily.

Choose a few promises and carry them with you. Speak them to yourself when fear stirs. Mediate on them and cherish them in your heart when despair presses in. The Word doesn't sink in all at once; it seeps slowly, through reflection and meditation, like water soaking deep into thirsty soil, nourishing the roots of your soul.

Jesus Himself gave us words we can build our lives on: *"...lo,*

I am with you alway, even unto the end of the world" (Matthew 28:20). In another instance, He said, *"I will not leave you comfortless: I will come to you"* (John 14:18). He does not waver. He does not add conditions. He is with you *always*.

So when pain overwhelms and emotions betray you, cling to what He has already spoken. His Word is steady when everything else feels unstable. His promises are faithful because His character is faithful. Though you may not feel Him, and though your heart may be broken, you can trust that He holds you. Let His promises be the well you return to again and again, so your soul remembers that you are not abandoned.

God gave you His Word long before this season touched your life. And that Word is enough. So let this season also be a time to listen. To listen closely to the God who has already spoken.

DRINK FROM THE WELL

If you are in a season of suffering and despair right now, do not sit passively and let loneliness or doubt take over. Run to God. Draw near to Him before those voices take root.

Move toward Him anyway, and talk with Him. Open your Bible and read, even if it feels stale or too heavy. Write a promise on a sticky note and put it where you will see it often. Take one small act of trust.

It may not feel refreshing at first. But drink anyway. Keep coming back to the well. Let His Word refresh you day after day, so hope has room to seep in. Emotions will follow faith, but rarely do they lead.

Do not give up. Bring your hurt to Christ. Surrender to the

work of waiting. Allow this season to draw you into deeper reliance on Him. Hold fast to the promises He has already given you.

One day, you will see what now feels hidden. You will look back and realize His presence never left you. Every tear, every restless night, every unanswered prayer will find its place in His story for you.

Until then, keep drinking from the well.

Keep believing.

7

THE PURPOSE OF IT ALL

Some truths can only be learned when life stops making sense and everything you thought was steady begins to shake. I used to see suffering as an interruption, a painful roadblock keeping me from the life I wanted. But I have come to see that pain, as unwelcome as it is, can lead us places comfort never could.

When heartbreak or hardship doesn't seem to end, when others go on with their lives while you're still sitting in the ache, questions rise like, *Why me? Where is God in this? Does He see what's happening?*

We have all heard people say statements like: "God is growing your character" or "He's working something good out of this." Those may be true, yet when you are the one hurting, it is not as comforting in that moment. What we long for is the presence of someone willing to enter the pain with us, to steady us when the ground gives way.

When suffering hits, our first instinct is often to brace

ourselves, to figure out how we'll survive the moment. We scan for answers, search for ways to make it stop, look for someone to hold us up. And often, that is exactly where the deeper work begins.

If God is loving, why does He allow pain? I have asked that more times than I can count. I have watched people I love suffer. We've all wrestled with grief and unanswered prayer, in one way or another. Yet in all of it, one truth has remained: God never wastes suffering. Nothing we endure slips past His care.

Suffering is not a detour; it is part of the story, a carefully placed piece in a picture we cannot yet see. God may not give us every answer, but He gives us His presence, His steady hand, and His strength.

Through fire, He refines. Through sorrow, He softens. Through every tear, He shapes compassion and strength within us. And in time, we discover that suffering has deepened us, teaching us to love, listen, and walk more gently with others in pain.

REFINED BY THE FIRE:
HOW SUFFERING GROWS US

I have never met anyone who grew deeper in their faith when life is at ease. We may thank God on the mountaintop, but we come to know Him in the valleys. Comfort doesn't stretch us, and ease rarely deepens us. But suffering transforms everything.

It is in the ache of hardship, when the prayers go unanswered and the pain refuses to lift, that something deep within us begins to shift.

James, the half-brother of Jesus, wrote something that sounds almost outrageous…until you have lived it: *"Count it all joy when ye fall into divers temptations; Knowing this, that the trying of your faith worketh patience…"* (James 1:2-3).

We find joy in trials because we begin to see what God is doing through them. James isn't telling us to minimize what hurts, nor is he saying to pretend everything is fine. He is offering something better, a way to *see* our trials differently, not as obstacles, but as opportunities for growth. It is a pathway to spiritual maturity that comfort cannot provide.

If you have walked with God through hardship, you already know that pain changes your prayers and humbles your pride. It strips away distractions and teaches you to cling to God as your only lifeline.

This is not just true for us, it is exemplified in the life of Jesus. Even He walked the hard road. His suffering was not forced upon Him, yet He chose it, embracing the path of surrendered intimacy with the Father. In His example, we see that suffering, when surrendered in love, can draw us closer to God in ways comfort never could.

WHEN LOVE LEADS TO SUFFERING

Some of the deepest suffering we will ever endure does not come from persecution or failure, but from love.

Think of the parents raising a child with special needs. The strength required each day is staggering: sleepless nights, sudden meltdowns, medical appointments, isolation. Just making it through meals or school calls can feel like climbing a mountain. The sacrifices are endless. And yet they keep going because of love.

Real love always costs something. It stretches your patience, drains your energy, and brings you face-to-face with your limits. But strangely, it is in that exhaustion where something sacred begins to grow. Through love's suffering, God forms meekness, nurtures compassion, and deepens our dependence on Him.

Over time, those parents become living reflections of Christ's tenderness. Their pain forms a gentleness and grace that touches everyone around them.

Perhaps your story is not about parenting. Maybe it is a strained marriage. An injustice that still troubles you. A chronic illness. Or the long, weary road of caring for someone who no longer knows your name.

Whatever the form, love can lead us straight into suffering, and it is not wasted. Look back at your life. Think of the seasons that cost you the most, the ones that left you breathless. Weren't those the same seasons that revealed something deeper in you that God had been shaping all along? A tenderness you didn't have before? A strength you did not know you carried? A clearer glimpse of God you had never seen?

Suffering has a way of stripping away what is shallow. It reveals what is eternal. Over time, it softens us. It teaches us how to love, not with expectations, but with grace.

THE LOSS THAT NEARLY BROKE ME

In 2014, my younger brother ended his life. Nothing prepares you for the suddenness and pain of that kind of moment. One day, he was here. The next, he was gone. The phone call. The disbelief that followed. And then the grief, crashing in like waves that never seemed to let up, soaking me to my core and making it hard to catch my breath at times.

I did not want to talk to anyone. I did not want comfort. I wanted answers. The pain was too raw and too personal. And the questions came like accusations, from something called survivor's guilt: *Why didn't I see it coming? Why didn't I do something?*

I did not know it at the time, but that was fear, shame, stigma, and pain at work, clinging to sorrow, pressing down, and telling me to disappear. That is what I wanted to do: hide and bury my anguish beneath a forced smile and busy schedule.

But God had other plans. A friend showed up while I was wallowing in the darkness, and instead of offering advice, he was simply present and listened to what I had to say. He did not try to fix me. He just sat beside me in my pain. And somehow, in that simple companionship, the first light of hope and healing began to seep through.

We rarely talk about how suffering can be twisted by Satan to isolate us, insinuating, *You're alone. No one understands. Stay shut up.* But what if that very pain, the thing you fear will drive people away, is precisely what God wants to use to draw others in?

Isaiah spoke of the Messiah who would come *"to bind up the brokenhearted"* and *"to comfort all that mourn"* (Isaiah 61:1–2). The comfort God pours into us through Christ is never meant to stay with us alone. He binds our wounds so that, in time, we can help comfort others with the same comfort we've received. That is both a mission and a lifeline. Your broken heart, when surrendered to Him, can become someone else's rescue rope.

Since my brother's death, I have met others standing at the edge of despair, beautiful souls battling suicidal thoughts and folks buried in grief. I have sat across from them with nothing more than my presence. I rarely have answers, but more importantly, I have two ears to listen, and a few gentle resources and love God has placed in my hands.

When you give back your suffering to God, it becomes a ministry. It sends you out into the world, empowered with a calling, along with empathy and the power of your presence.

Your scars do not disqualify you from service or ministry. They make you real and relatable. And they may be precisely what gives someone else the courage to believe healing is possible. There is a unique power in shared experience. Who better to offer hope to someone adjusting to life with a disability or to support a grieving parent than someone who has walked that same path?

When we have lived through a struggle, we gain an ability to empathize and credibility that no textbook or well-meaning advice can match. This is where pain becomes purpose. Our deepest wounds can be a source of hope and healing for others, where God begins to turn suffering into something sacred.

WHEN EVERYTHING FALLS APART

There was a season when I lost my home, my finances, and the sense of security I once took for granted. I went from stability to sleeping in my car, unsure where my next meal would come from or how long I could keep pretending I was okay.

Shame clung to me, and it was suffocating. I did not want anyone to know. I did not even know how to pray. I felt helpless and painfully alone in a world that praises "strength" and celebrates "success." In moments like that, failure never feels temporary; it feels like a judgment, a mark of weakness, even a moral flaw.

Suffering has a way of shattering the illusion of control in our lives. When life is comfortable, we lean on our skills, our routines, and our resources. But when the bottom drops out, those supports crumble, and suddenly you're left exposed with no safety net, no backup plan, and no answers. You are left with only one question: *Now what?*

It was in that shattered place that I encountered the tender mercy of God. With nothing left to cling to, I began to notice people I had once overlooked. I saw pain in strangers' faces. I stopped measuring my worth by what I had owned or achieved. Living with so little taught me what contentment really is. My joy was no longer tied to comfort but rooted in God's nearness and the unexpected gifts He gives, even in the midst of a challenging season.

Suffering remade me. Slowly, God built a different kind of strength in me that only grows from letting go and saying, "God, I can't...but You can."

If you are in that place now, hold on. God's goodness is still at work in ways you cannot yet see, shaping strength from your surrender and beauty from the fragments of your brokenness.

A PECULIAR KIND OF PRAISE

Some moments in suffering defy explanation. They do not make sense to the mind or the heart. One of those moments came as I watched my mother endure unspeakable pain. Over the years, she had already faced chronic ailments, exhausting treatments, and endless setbacks. But this time was different. A doctor prescribed an inappropriate medication. He treated her like a test subject, and what followed was two agonizing weeks of pain so intense I still struggle to talk about it.

I remember her cries and standing beside her bed, helpless, as she writhed and wept, begging God for relief. And the worst part was that the doctor refused to listen. Her suffering was dismissed as if it were nothing.

Yet one afternoon, something sacred happened. Her body trembling and her voice barely audible, she uttered through the pain, "I guess… God… wants me… to understand… a little… of what Jesus… suffered… for me." And in that place of agony, she began to worship— shouting raw and piercing praise to the LORD. She worshipped because she still trusted Him. Somehow, her anguish became a doorway into deeper fellowship with God.

That moment will stay with me forever. In her anguish and worship, I witnessed a truth unfold before my eyes: God, in His mercy, allows our pain to reveal hidden treasures of understanding that comfort never could teach: the depth of Christ's love, the cost of our redemption, and the joy that survives fire.

LETTING GO OF THE WHEEL

One of the hardest aspects of suffering is that it reveals our deep desire to stay in control. We spend so much of life trying to manage outcomes. Work harder, plan better, pray more, stay ahead, hoping everything will turn out the way we want. But suffering shatters that illusion, and suddenly we're face-to-face with something we do not like to admit: we were never really in control.

The reality is that we often build our lives around the illusion of control over our finances, our health, our relationships, and even how others perceive us. We curate our image and protect our reputation. And when those things begin to unravel, we panic and scramble, grasping at what feels secure.

But maybe that very unraveling is God's grace. It invites a pause, a period of honest reflection. How do you respond when life is clearly out of your hands? Have you ever cried, "I don't know what to do," or "I can't take this anymore"? If so, that confession might just be the beginning of something far more wonderful than control ever promised.

Scripture does not ask you to hold it all together. It invites you to trust the One who holds *you* together. *"A man's heart deviseth his way: but the LORD directeth his steps"* (Proverbs 16:9).

Control can unknowingly become an idol. Often it takes suffering to reveal just how tightly we have been clinging to our need for control. Like a skilled surgeon, God makes the necessary cut to heal what is wounded, buried, or misaligned.

That truth is hard to embrace. But God never asked you to carry the burden of control. That burden was never yours to bear. And if that sounds foreign, ask yourself whether you've believed that pleasing God means managing everything just right, or whether cultural Christianity convinced you that your worth comes from performance.

The gospel is simpler than that. God leads. We follow. That's it. So when the voices (even from well-meaning Christians) tell you to "Take control" or "Pull yourself together," remember that is not the message of Jesus.

WHEN SUFFERING FINDS A VOICE

The world tells us to avoid suffering at all costs. Chase comfort, numb the ache, distract, escape, and move on. Honestly, it is tempting because pain hurts. It interrupts our rhythm and drains our strength. No one wants to suffer.

But the Bible offers a promise: if God allows hardship to happen in your life, He intends to transform the pain, the loss, and every difficulty into something good. In the midst of suffering, it's natural to focus only on wanting the problem gone. Yet if we trust Him through it, we can look back later and see that His hand was at work the entire time. Then we can say, "This is what You were doing. You made me wait... and wow, look at what You accomplished."

God never guaranteed an easy life. But He did promise His presence. He may not remove the hardship, but He always walks through it with us. And when suffering is yielded to God, it begins to tell the story of where God met us at our weakest. It shows others what grace looks like in real life.

To suffer is part of being human. When it comes, and it will, we often scramble, reaching for meds, money, distractions, anything to stop the bleeding. But those remedies do not heal. A full stomach empties again. A beautiful purchase loses its shine. Even a temporary high fades, leaving you emptier than before.

The enemy knows this. That's why he keeps offering little lies wrapped in promises: *If you just had more... looked better... achieved more...felt better...you'd be okay.* But it is not true. Some of the most admired, accomplished people are secretly miserable, and do not know how to escape it.

But as followers of Christ, we do not pretend that "bad things only happen to good people." No, good and bad circumstances happen to everyone. Satan is an equal-opportunity destroyer. But our God is a relentless Redeemer.

And that makes all the difference. You carry the presence of a living Saviour who suffered first so He could walk with you now. To believe that *"all things work together for good"* means you are convinced that even the worst hardships can be redeemed for God's glory *and* for your good.

So lean into Christ. Do not see your suffering as punishment but as holy ground, where grace finds you, where love holds you, and where God speaks. As you surrender, saying, "Here I am, Lord—even in my weakness," you become a vessel through which His power flows. The pain may not vanish, but it will not be wasted. In God's hands, your testimony can become a force for good that brings light to a world in desperate need. Let God give your suffering a voice.

8

TRIAL OR PUNISHMENT?

Have you ever whispered in the darkest moments, "Is God punishing me?" If so, you are not alone. I have too, along with countless others before us. One of the most striking moments in Scripture illustrates just how deeply that question resonates within all of us and how powerfully Jesus responds. So, let's step back to a dusty afternoon in Jerusalem, where a man's story and the Saviour's words would forever change the way we see suffering.

The city was alive that day. Merchants called from their stalls, children frolicked between carts, and sandals scraped across the stone road. But along the edge of the bustling streets sat one man, blind since birth. Some called him cursed. Others shook their heads with pity. Almost everyone believed that his blindness must have been caused by sin, either his own or his parents'.

When Jesus and His disciples passed by, even they echoed the assumptions everyone else believed.

"Master," the disciples asked, *"who did sin, this man, or his*

parents, that he was born blind?" (John 9:2).

What a question to ask. I wonder how many times the blind man overheard that same accusation muttered about him, planting doubt in his heart: *Did I deserve this? Was I born broken because God is angry with me?*

But then Jesus speaks, and His words break through the unnecessary weight humankind had been carrying for centuries: *"Neither hath this man sinned, nor his parents:"* Jesus answered, *"but that the works of God should be made manifest in him"* (John 9:3).

Then, Jesus healed him. Just like that, the narrative that had shadowed this man's life was undone. Jesus not only gave him sight; He gave him dignity. He declared that not all suffering is punishment, and that pain is not always the fruit of sin. His blindness was not divine payback, but divine purpose. It was an opening for the glory of God to break through in a way no one could have imagined.

I have never sat blind on a roadside, but I have wrestled with questions just as profound. I have wondered if my pain was punishment. I have carried shame that felt unbearable.

For me, it has surfaced in various ways over the years. One of the hardest came during my adolescence, even into my late teens, when I battled chronic bed-wetting. Morning after morning, I woke in shame, thinking, *"God... is this because of something I did?"* I never dared to voice it aloud, but the guilt throbbing in my chest was loud enough. Even when my mind knew better, my heart kept circling back to that same fear.

You may know that feeling, too. Maybe you're carrying something right now, and you have wondered if God is punishing you. If so, please know that your suffering is not proof of His anger.

Sometimes it is simply the fallout of living in a broken world. But shame is not for you to bear, nor are you resigned to condemnation.

We follow a Saviour who never wields pain to humiliate His children. If God were still punishing us for sins Jesus already paid for, then what was the point of the cross? Instead, He uses even the hardest struggles to reveal His glory and bring hope where we least expect it.

REWRITING THE SIN-AND-CONSEQUENCE NARRATIVE

Sin has consequences, sometimes devastating ones. But consequences are not the same as punishment. A man who neglects his health for years may suffer physically, but that does not mean God is angry with him. It simply means we live in a world of cause and effect, and our choices have consequences. The same is true in relationships: if we betray trust or walk away from God's ways, the fallout is not divine revenge but the natural outcome of paths we choose to walk.

In my early twenties, I was angry at God. I wanted nothing to do with church or Christians, so I walked away. For nearly three years, I lived life on my own terms. Outwardly, I seemed fine. I ran a business, earned good money, and kept myself entertained, but inside, I was miserable. I felt empty, disconnected from God, and hungry for something deeper than comfort or success could ever offer.

My misery was the natural emptiness that comes from living apart from the Source of life. The consequences were the reality of life without Him. And yet, even in that place, God did not give up. He pursued me patiently. He allowed the weight of my choices to humble me, not destroy me. Through that season, He drew me back, closer than I had ever been before.

The prophet Isaiah described our condition perfectly: *"All we like sheep have gone astray; we have turned every one to his own way..."* (Isaiah 53:6). We wander, insisting on our own path. And when the consequences hit, it is easy to cry out, "Why is God doing this to me?"

Much of our suffering is tangled with pride, the stubborn belief that we know better. Even when the warning signs flash like red lights, we barrel forward, convinced we can handle it on our own... or that somehow, we can escape the consequences.

That is the danger of self-reliance. It blinds us. It convinces us we wield the power, even as everything unravels around us. When the fallout comes, we can quickly assume God is punishing us. But God is not out to crush you. He is the Shepherd who sees you wandering and longs to bring you home. Even when we stray far, He pursues us with gentle nudges and unmistakable signs, and always with love.

He wants to free us from the pain our choices bring. He wants us to experience a life abundantly without regret. That's the heart of a Father, not a judge.

SIN AND DISCIPLINE

There is something about comfort that lulls us into forgetting who we are. When life is smooth, the career is on track, everything at home seems fine, and your best-laid plans are falling into place, it is easy to believe we are in control. Comfort lulls us into thinking, *You've got this.* And slowly, we stop depending on God because, truthfully, we do not feel we need Him.

Pride rarely storms into our lives. More often, it sneaks in subtly, almost politely. Especially if we've been around church long enough to avoid the "big" sins, we can begin thinking we're doing *quite fine*. Outwardly, everything looks clean. Inwardly, something toxic may be spreading.

The Bible calls this "the deceitfulness of sin." Often, it is not a massive scandal but something that settles in quietly, like a tapeworm in the heart, hidden, feeding and draining us over time. A trace of resentment. A hint of judgment. A touch of entitlement. And before long, we're spiritually sick, even while we keep showing up to the church house, volunteering in ministry, and looking the part.

When sin or pride takes root, God does not punish us. But He does care enough to discipline us. And there's a world of difference between the two. Punishment flows from wrath. Discipline flows from love—it restores. Punishment was already placed on Christ at the cross. God no longer responds to His children as a judge but as a Father who corrects in order to restore, never to harm.

He isn't lashing out at you. He is calling you back. Just as a parent corrects a child to protect and form them, God disciplines us because we belong to Him.

The writer of Hebrews puts it this way: *"My son, despise not thou the chastening of the LORD, nor faint when thou art rebuked of him: For whom the LORD loveth he chasteneth, and scourgeth every son whom he receiveth...if ye be without chastisement, whereof all are partakers, then are ye bastards, and not sons"* (Hebrews 12:5-8).

God's discipline is proof that you are His child. Of course, it never feels pleasant. Discipline can be confusing and even painful. But here's the paradox: that very discomfort may be the most unmistakable evidence of His care. If He did not care, He would let you wander unchecked. But His love refuses to leave you there.

When we keep choosing our own way instead of His way, God often lets us feel the sting of our choices to wake us up. Pain has a way of opening our eyes when pride has closed them. Still, His heart does not change. He's not condemning you; He is calling you. He doesn't discipline to harm, but to heal and build you up.

And sometimes, the refining has nothing to do with rebellion, but with the battle for our faith itself. Take, for example, bold, passionate Peter on the night Jesus was arrested. Jesus told him, *"Simon, Simon, behold, Satan hath desired to have you, that he may sift you as wheat: But I have prayed for thee, that thy faith fail not"* (Luke 22:31-32).

The imagery is striking. Just as wheat is beaten and tossed to separate grain from chaff, Peter, too, would be shaken to the core. His failure was coming—and it would cut deep. He would deny Jesus three times. And yet, Jesus was not casting Peter aside. He was preparing him for restoration. The sifting was not to undo him, but to prepare him for the future that God had planned. Peter's failure became the soil where humility and dependence could grow, preparing him for everything God would later do through him.

And do you remember what Jesus did after the resurrection? He sought Peter out. Jesus restored him. And that same man, now humbled, would become one of the boldest leaders in the early church. That is what discipline does. It refines, not rejects. It humbles, but never destroys.

So, if you are in a season of pain, ask yourself: *Could God be trying to get my attention? Could this be His love expressed through correction rather than punishment?* Know that God disciplines those He loves. And you, my friend, are deeply, unshakably loved.

NOT BECAUSE OF SIN, BUT…NOT

What if, instead of reacting with dread or resentment, we began to listen to our suffering as a teacher? I do not mean embracing it with some twisted desire for pain. I am talking about receiving it as a mysterious gift from God, which He uses to help us mature and grow. This is what Jesus meant when He said, *"…let him deny himself, and take up his cross daily, and follow me"* (Luke 9:23). Taking up your cross does not mean chasing suffering. It means letting go of control, laying down pride, and choosing surrender each day, allowing hardship to reveal what keeps us from knowing Him more fully.

The Bible offers powerful imagery to help us understand this process; one of the clearest is that of fire. In Malachi 3, God is described as a refiner, patiently tending the fire and removing the impurities from silver so that what remains is pure. That process isn't gentle. It separates, leaving only what truly belongs.

In the same way, suffering purifies us: exposing our pride, humbling ambition, and leading us back to dependence on God. It refines the heart in ways comfort never could.

But not all refining comes through fire. Sometimes, it comes through something more personal: a thorn in one's side. And in Paul's story, we find a thorn that is persistent, painful, and, yes, necessary.

Paul never tells us exactly what his thorn was. Perhaps it was a physical condition or a mental struggle. Or it could have been opposition from others. Whatever it was, he begged God to remove it three times. Each time, God said no. It wasn't that He did not care. The thorn had a purpose.

Paul writes, *"Lest I should be exalted above measure... there was given to me a thorn"* (2 Corinthians 12:7). It wasn't punishment. It was mercy, a divine safeguard against pride and a reminder that strength comes through weakness, and that weakness draws us closer to Christ.

I have to admit, I wish I could learn humility and dependence on God without pain. I wish I could stay close to Christ without hardship. But on this side of Heaven, it just doesn't seem to work that way. The only people untouched by suffering are those who have given themselves over to chasing comfort, power, and pleasure. They numb their souls to the voice of God so they can live life on their own terms. Outwardly, they might look successful. But inwardly, something is slowly dying.

That is the danger of resisting suffering; it can mean resisting Christ. And in doing so, we miss the very reason we were created, which is to walk in fellowship with the living God.

Suffering will come. The question isn't *if*, but *how* we will face it, with or without Jesus. In that fire, and with that thorn, we find Him as a present Redeemer who walks beside us and refines us from the inside out.

TO KNOW CHRIST

No discussion of suffering would be complete without looking to Jesus, who endured more than anyone else. He did not just teach about pain; He lived it. From His first breath to His final cry, Jesus faced affliction. He walked through every oppression: mockery, abandonment, slander, hunger, thirst, weariness, betrayal, and ultimately, crucifixion, though He had done no wrong. And through it all, He never wavered in His trust in the Father.

To His contemporaries, His life and His claim to be God seemed incompatible. How could the immortal and all-powerful God take on a life marked by weakness and pain? Shouldn't the Son of God be bathed in comfort, honor and admiration?

But God's definition of glory stands in sharp contrast to the world's shallow and often punitive view. Jesus turned every human expectation upside down. He taught people to pray for their enemies, to bless those who cursed them, to walk the extra mile, and to turn the other cheek. He praised the faith of the outsider, elevated the lowly, and told stories in which the hero was a despised Samaritan and devotion came from a poor widow.

He lived what He preached. He embraced suffering of every kind, not because He deserved it, but because we did. Isaiah 53:5 says, *"He was wounded for our transgressions, he was bruised for our iniquities: the chastisement of our peace was upon him; and with his stripes we are healed."*

He took our punishment. He absorbed our shame and condemnation. And in return, Christ gave us His righteousness. Jesus suffered so we could know Him—not from a distance, but in the depths of our need. Suffering is part of our human experience, and within it God teaches us to trust Him more deeply, repent more honestly, and surrender more freely, until His glory becomes the desire of our hearts.

Jesus lived, died, and rose again to give us renewed hope amid our pain. Until we get to Heaven, we will never be completely free from sin, never fully whole. Yet every time we suffer with Him, we are shaped more into His likeness. Every act of surrender draws us closer to the heart of God. Joy is found not in escaping the fire, but in walking through it with the One who gave everything to make us His.

WALKING IN FREEDOM

Thanks to Christ, we are no longer slaves to sin. The cross broke the chains that once bound us, and through His resurrection, we have been offered new life. Romans 6:6 reminds us: *"our old man is crucified with him... that henceforth we should not serve sin."* In other words, we do not have to live the way we used to. We are no longer ruled by shame, guilt, or cycles we once couldn't break.

And we did not earn this freedom either. It is a gift. A few verses later, we're told, *"For sin shall not have dominion over you: for ye are not under the law, but under grace"* (v. 14). That is what real freedom looks like. It is not a license to sin, but grace-powered strength to walk differently.

Grace enables us to be grateful, and gratitude opens the door to transformation because the Holy Spirit is alive within us. Jesus freed us to live a life that glorifies God, a life marked by peace and purpose, even when everything else is falling apart. But sin always steals that peace. Even subtle rebellion leaves us restless; guilt creeps in, relationships suffer, and slowly we disconnect from the life God intended for us.

Yet Romans 6:18 gloriously affirms, *"Being then made free from sin, ye became the servants of righteousness."* We weren't set free to return to old chains; we have been called to walk in a new life that brings a peace that passes understanding. This isn't a call for perfection (we'll mess up and wander at times) but an opportunity to walk in right fellowship with God. Under grace, our hearts find rest. We stop striving and begin choosing what nourishes our souls instead of what wounds them.

If you find yourself suffering from sin you've ignored, then this is a gentle, but urgent, call to repentance. It is far from a shameful scolding (believe me, I'm the last person who should be scolding anyway); it is an invitation to return to God.

Begin by being honest with God. Grieve the sin because it has wounded your closeness with Him and others. Ask for cleansing. Repentance is meant to be a realignment of the heart. It says, "Lord, I want to walk in step with You again."

Repentance also means making amends with others for wrongs. To paraphrase Matthew 5:23-24, Jesus said that if someone has something against you, go and reconcile first. Mending broken relationships matters deeply to God. Without it, repentance leaves a fracture in the body of Christ. But when we ask for forgiveness and seek to repair what is broken, the weight inside us lifts, peace returns, and shame loses its grip.

Jesus offers not a life without pain, but one full of peace, purpose, and joy. A life where guilt no longer defines you, shame no longer binds you, and repentance becomes the doorway to freedom, allowing you to walk in the light restored, whole, and unafraid.

FREEDOM IN CHRIST ALONE

As we step back and look at all the many faces of suffering, one liberating truth emerges: in Christ, we are not only forgiven, we are being remade. Your suffering is not a sign that God has turned His back on you. It is not a verdict of guilt. More often, it is an invitation from God to let Him shape the deepest parts of who you are.

Sometimes our suffering comes from sin we've refused to surrender. Sometimes it comes simply from living in a fallen world. But none of it is wasted in the hands of the One who makes all things new.

That's the power of grace. Jesus does not only save us from the penalty of sin, He saves us from the prison of shame, freeing us from the relentless cycle of hiding, pretending, and striving. He leads us into a life of deep, abiding peace that does not depend on perfect circumstances, but on a perfect Saviour. And in that peace, we discover that suffering never gets the final word; redemption does.

When we bring our pain, repentance, and broken places to Jesus, He meets us with compassion. He walks with us through the fire. He restores what was lost. He transforms what was broken. And He calls us forward as sons and daughters who walk in freedom.

So, whether your suffering today is refining you, disciplining you, or simply reminding you that this world is not your home, hold fast. Let it draw you nearer to Christ: humbling, purifying, awakening you, and shaping you into His likeness. The goal is not merely to feel better, but to be made whole. And in Jesus, that is exactly what is happening.

PART II

When Suffering Strikes

9

DISAPPOINTMENT: SHATTERED EXPECTATIONS

Have you ever faced a disappointment so deep that it felt like the ground gave way beneath your feet and all you could do was fall? Maybe it was a betrayal you never saw coming, a diagnosis that shattered the future you had imagined, or someone you loved walked away without explanation. Or perhaps it wasn't one massive blow at all, but a series of smaller hits that slowly weakened the scaffolding of hope beneath you. Whatever it was, it shook you, and something inside you gave way.

Disappointment affects us in big ways. It stops our momentum, clouds our vision, and makes joy feel like a stranger. You walk toward what looks like an open door, and suddenly, it slams shut. And there you are, staring at it in stunned silence, unsure what just happened and where to go next.

In that hush, questions about God can begin to surface. *Did I miss His will? Did I do something wrong?* Those are the moments when faith feels fragile, when everything you thought you understood starts to unravel. The gap between expectation and reality can feel impossibly wide.

But friend, God does not leave us in the gap. He meets us there. He does not waste the pain of disappointment; even through it, He is working faithfully, offering a way forward. I am not speaking of a shortcut, but a steady and sacred path that begins with honesty and leads toward healing and hope.

And that's where we begin in this chapter: with a God who still writes beautiful stories out of broken hopes.

WHEN EXPECTATIONS GO UNMET

Disappointment usually begins with a hope we were holding onto or a future we believed would come to pass. Maybe it was prayer we lifted with faith, a promise we felt sure about, or a future we were walking toward with confidence. Disappointment is what happens when those hopes go unmet.

And let's be honest: we all have expectations. A wife expects her husband to be faithful. A friend expects loyalty. A follower of Christ naturally hopes that years of obedience will bear some fruit. These are not selfish desires; they are often healthy, good, and even biblical.

But problems arise when our expectations are shaped more by our longings rather than by God's promises. We expect healing, yet sickness remains. We expect open doors, but they keep closing. We expect decency, yet betrayal comes instead. When that happens, sadness and disorientation settle in. What once seemed certain suddenly doesn't make sense. We thought we understood how life works and how God moves…but now we aren't so sure.

That's when the real wrestling with "what it all means" begins. Questions dig into your theology and your trust: *Did I misunderstand God? Did I put my hope in the wrong thing? Can I still trust Him?*

These moments are painful, but they can also be sacred. Disappointment, as much as it hurts, can lead us into a deeper trust built not on what God *does for us*, but on who He *is*. Unmet hopes and expectations do not have to derail us. They can refine us. They can strip away illusions and invite us to anchor our hope not in outcomes but in the One who never changes.

WHAT EXPECTATIONS *AREN'T*

Sometimes disappointment can come from misunderstood expectations, blessings we assumed God would do simply because we longed for them so much. And when they don't happen, we feel shaken to our core.

I have been there. I expected healing because I prayed hard and trusted God with all my heart. I expected certain dreams to unfold because I worked diligently. I expected relationships to last because I loved sincerely and gave them everything I had. But then life took a different turn, and I was left wondering, *Did God let me down? Or did I just assume He said something He never actually promised?*

Those are hard questions to sit with. But here's the truth I have had to learn slowly and often painfully, I'll admit: many of the assumptions I mistook for promises from God were actually expectations dressed in spiritual language. God is always faithful, but He is not obligated to fulfill the hopes we script for ourselves. He is not a vending machine, dispensing blessings in exchange for our good behavior. He is a sovereign, loving Father who leads by wisdom, not by wish lists.

That does not mean we stop hoping. But it does mean taking a closer look at what our hope is anchored to. Are we trusting in what God actually said or in what we wish He would do?

I have made that mistake before, confusing sincerity with certainty. I have thought, *Surely God will do this. I've done everything right.* But faith does not mean convincing God to follow our plan. It means trusting Him even when His plan looks nothing like ours.

God is not trying to rob us of joy. He is protecting us from anchoring our hope in fragile priorities. He wants our hearts rooted in something deeper and more eternal than outcomes: *Himself.*

When the dream collapses and the prayers seem unanswered, His goodness remains. His character does not change. And He is at work, even when we do not yet understand how.

THE DOORWAY OF DISAPPOINTMENT

Disappointment often feels like a dead end. A door closes. A dream dies. And we're left staring at the pieces of what we imagined life would be, wishing we could turn back and make sense of what went wrong.

But what if disappointment is not a wall? What if it is a doorway?

Sometimes, the very thing we see as a setback is actually a redirection. At first, it may feel cruel and confusing. But with time, we begin to see that the closed door protected us from what we could not yet see, or prepared us for what we were not ready to receive.

Time is one of the greatest tools God designed. Heaven exists outside time, yet God placed us within time to teach, guide, and reveal His purposes through slow, unfolding seasons. Waiting is difficult because it asks us to hold onto hope, surrender, and endurance all at once.

Sometimes disappointment strikes so hard that it feels unbearable. Yet when it passes, we find ourselves changed; perhaps sadder, yes, but wiser, more grounded, more aware, and maybe even more surrendered.

Time also has a way of softening pain. What feels like devastation in one season often becomes clarity in the next. Obstacles that once seemed insurmountable turn into turning points. Disappointments become soil for something greater to grow, like faith, patience, endurance, and dependence. These are the qualities we rarely ask for, but desperately need.

God does not rush His work. He allows us to sit in confusing seasons because He knows the fruit they will produce. He most certainly is not trying to make us suffer needlessly. Waiting stretches us, strips away layers of self-reliance, and teaches us to depend entirely on Him. We learn to wait, not only for outcomes, but on the Lord Himself, and discover that He alone is enough.

So, when your dreams die, expectations go unmet, or disappointment leaves you reeling, pause. Take the opportunity to bow before the Lord. Acknowledge your ache. Sit with it in His presence. Grieve if you need to. Bring it to Jesus with open hands, and ask, *What are You forming in me through this loss? What do I need to learn, Lord?*

Then… listen. You may not like what is happening. You may not understand it. But with God, disappointment doesn't have to be a wall. It can be a doorway into deeper trust, greater purpose, and into a joy you never imagined.

YOU'RE NOT THE FIRST

Disappointment has a way of isolating us. In our lowest of low moments, it tells us big lies: *You're the only one who's ever felt this way. No one else has been through what you're going through. No one would understand.* And before long, our pain turns inward. We withdraw. We second-guess ourselves. Shame creeps in. Loneliness settles like a fog.

But that voice is not from God.

You are certainly not the first to wrestle with unmet hopes. The pages of Scripture are full of men and women who carried unanswered prayers, lingering heartache, and dreams delayed far beyond their patience. Through their stories, we find comfort and perspective.

Think of Sarai, Abram's wife. She waited for years, barren, heartbroken, and longing for a child. Yet God was not late. He was preparing her faith for a miracle that would echo through generations.

Think of David, a young man anointed king yet tested by relentless trials. Years of hiding, filled with uncertainties and personal struggles, drew him to pour out his heart in psalms, crying, *"How long, O Lord?"* His disappointments did not disqualify him; they prepared him to lead with strength, humility, dependence on God, and a heart after God's own.

Think of Elijah, fresh off a mountaintop victory. He called down fire from heaven and slew hundreds of false prophets, and yet days later, fear and exhaustion sent him fleeing into the wilderness.

Collapsing beneath a broom tree, he cried out, *"It is enough, Lord. Take my life."* Yet God responded not with rebuke, but with rest, nourishment, and gentle guidance.

Think of John the Baptist, the bold, fearless forerunner of Christ. He, too, struggled with disappointment. After being imprisoned for his obedience, he sent messengers to ask Jesus, "Are you the One, or should we look for another?" Jesus did not scold him. He reassured him: *The blind receive their sight, and the lame walk, the lepers are cleansed, and the deaf hear, the dead are raised up, and the poor have the gospel preached to them"* (Matthew 11:5). While God's work did not look the way John expected, His plan was unfolding faithfully.

Over and over, God has shown up for His people, and He will not abandon you. Disappointment does not disqualify you, nor does it signal that God has turned away. Just as He guided Sarai, sustained Elijah, and strengthened John, He still walks closely with you today.

So when doubt creeps in, let the Bible remind you that you are in remarkable company. You are not the first to struggle. The same God who carried the faithful through their lowest moments carries you now. Just as He wrote their stories with hope and purpose, He is still at work, crafting your story far grander than what you can see.

WE MAY BE DISAPPOINTED, BUT GOD IS NOT

Sometimes the hardest disappointments come after years of faithfulness, perhaps when we assumed the most difficult seasons were behind us. When years of pouring yourself out leave you feeling spent, as though the window of possibility has closed and all that remains is the ache of what might have been. Few stories illustrate this better than Moses's.

He walked with God in a way few others ever have. He heard God's voice from the burning bush. He bravely stood before Pharaoh. He parted the Red Sea, received the Ten Commandments carved by God's own finger, and led a nation through the wilderness. Scripture says the Lord spoke with him face to face, as one speaks with a friend (Exodus 33:11). He wasn't just a prophet; he was a friend of God.

And yet, after all those years of obedience, one moment of frustration changed everything. In Numbers 20, the people complained again about needing water, and God instructed Moses to speak to the rock. But weary and angry, Moses struck the rock instead. Water still gushed forth, yet the consequences were sobering. God said: *"Because ye believed me not, to sanctify me in the eyes of the children of Israel, therefore ye shall not bring this congregation into the land which I have given them"* (vs. 12).

At first glance, it seems severe. Could one misstep really keep Moses from the Promised Land? But God was not punishing out of wrath. He was revealing a deeper story. The first time water was needed, God commanded Moses to strike the rock. That rock, Paul later identified as Christ (1 Corinthians 10:4). Jesus, the Rock, would be struck once for our sins, which was enough. His suffering did not need repetition.

This second time, God said to speak to the rock—not strike it. Why? Because the cross was complete. After Jesus was struck, we are no longer called to earn grace; we are called to trust God in faith. Moses' outburst became a symbol of human striving, trying to perform what God had already accomplished through grace. It misrepresented God before the people, and that is what kept Moses from entering the Promised Land.

Yet God was not finished with Moses. His failure did not cancel God's love. His disappointment did not erase God's purpose. Moses was still called *"My servant."* He was taken to the mountaintop to see the land from afar—a final, grace-filled glimpse of what was to come. And centuries later, Moses stood on the Mount of Transfiguration not as a failed leader, but glorified, speaking with Jesus Himself beside Elijah.

The same Moses who could not cross over in life… crossed over in glory. That's who God is: merciful, just, and kind. Yes, He disciplines, but never discards. He corrects, but never condemns the one He loves.

So, if you are sitting in the silence of disappointment, thinking it's too late or that your mistake has written the final chapter, remember this: God is not disappointed in you. He sees the bigger story. And He's still writing it.

The grace that welcomed Moses into glory is the same grace walking with you now. The same Rock struck for your salvation still pours out living water. His grace is not running out. And the Promised Land you thought you missed? There may be more to come than you ever imagined.

SURRENDER YOUR EXPECTATIONS

One of the hardest lessons in the life of faith is to learn to let go of our expectations. We all carry them. Sometimes we voice them aloud, but more often they dwell buried in our hearts. Over time, they grow in our thoughts: *Surely, by now, I'd be married; God has to bless this ministry I've poured myself into; If I just pray harder, healing will definitely come.* The danger is subtle: when those hopes do not unfold as we imagined, disappointment creeps in. And left unchecked, it can harden into bitterness.

Jesus came to serve, but not to serve our comforts. He came to meet our deepest need: cleansing us of sin, drawing us into righteousness, and forming us into His likeness. Yet we often hand Him our plans and say, "Here, bless this," instead of asking, "Lord, what do You want for me?"

From my experience, I have learned that disappointment often comes from clinging to what we think we need. I have had to lay treasured dreams, longed-for opportunities, and prayers I poured myself into at Jesus' feet, walking away with empty hands. And yet, those empty hands were exactly what He was waiting to fill.

Disappointment comes from unmet hopes. Despair comes when we cling to them. That's why surrender matters so much: it is trust. Surrender is the moment we stop demanding God fit into our timeline and begin trusting that He is good, even when we cannot see the whole plan.

King Solomon captures it beautifully: *"Trust in the Lord with all thine heart; and lean not unto thine own understanding. In all thy ways acknowledge him, and he shall direct thy paths"* (Proverbs 3:5-6). Jeremiah offers a sobering reminder: *"The heart is deceitful above all things, and desperately wicked: who can know it?"* (Jeremiah 17:9). These verses caution us to hold our desires loosely and cling to the One who sees the whole picture.

So ask yourself: "Have I truly surrendered the dreams I cherish most, or am I still holding a blueprint in one hand, hoping God will bless what I've already designed?"

Surrender is never easy; it always costs. But it is in surrender that peace begins and joy returns. Even if God does not give you what you expected, He gives more of Himself. And sometimes that's the miracle we never saw coming.

WALKING WITH HOPE IN DISAPPOINTMENT

Disappointment has a way of pulling the rug out from under us. Plans fall apart. Prayers go unanswered. Dreams slip through our fingers. And we are left wondering, *What now?* But when we begin to see disappointment through the lens of faith, everything shifts. It is no longer the end of the story. It becomes an invitation to loosen our grip on what we thought life would be and to trust the Author who sees the story from beginning to end.

This kind of surrender involves placing ourselves fully in His hands. Instead of clinging to outcomes, we cling to the God who loves us. Instead of defining peace by how our plans *should* have turned out, we begin to believe that God is doing something better—something purposeful—even if we cannot see it yet.

No, it is not easy. The ache is real. Healing rarely comes quickly, and the journey is often long and slow. Yet the presence of pain does not mean the absence of God. He walks with us in the wilderness, sits beside us in the silence, dries our tears, and speaks comfort in ways words cannot capture.

When we surrender our expectations, space opens up for God to reshape our hearts, realign our hopes, and remind us of who He truly is: the God of grace, power, and unfailing love.

So, what do we do in the middle of it all? We allow ourselves to grieve. We bring our pain to Jesus with open hands. But we also make a conscious decision not to let our disappointment define us. It does not have the final say.

As we walk through the difficult places, we remember that we are not walking alone. The Scriptures are full of companions who wrestled with dashed hopes, yet in those very moments, they saw God more clearly as the One who never fails.

Walk slowly. Feel what you need to feel, but do not stop advancing. Disappointment may cloud the path, but it does not cancel the promise.

One day, what feels like the end will be revealed as the beginning of something deeper, something better. Keep your heart open. Keep your eyes fixed on Christ. Your story is still unfolding. And grace will have the final word.

10

THE WOUND OF BETRAYAL

Have you ever trusted someone, only to have them turn on you without warning? Not just anyone—but someone you welcomed into your home, someone who knew the depths of your heart. That is the sting of betrayal: the wound delivered not by an enemy, but by a friend.

When someone you trusted stabs you in the back, it leaves more than a wound. It leaves confusion. You replay conversations, wondering, *"Did I miss the signs? How could they do this to me?"* And it is not just the relationship that is broken. It is your sense of safety, your ability to trust, and even your peace of mind.

I have been there, and I've walked alongside many others who have been there, too: pastors betrayed by their deacons, spouses abandoned by the very person who promised to stand beside them for life, friends turned cold after years of fellowship. In those moments, I, and we all, often look up and ask, "Lord, where were You? Did You see this?"

Sometimes there is a long pause between our questions and God's answers. In that quiet stretch, the wound feels raw, and the silence feels personal. You don't just want reasons; you want reassurance. You want to know your heart wasn't foolish for loving, and that God hasn't stepped back from the wreckage. That is the place where betrayal hits its deepest point, not just in the loss of someone, but in the disorientation that follows. And it is often right there, in that unsettled space, that God begins to draw near in ways we could not see before.

If it feels like your heart bears this ache alone, take comfort in knowing that countless others across time and place have walked this same path of pain and confusion. The pages of Scripture are filled with God's people facing betrayal, heartbreak, and broken trust. You are in good company, and God sees your pain.

You can take heart: God saw it all. Every whispered word behind your back. Every heavy moment of silence left you feeling abandoned. Every tear that soaked your pillow. He has not turned away from your pain. What was broken is not beyond repair. There is still hope and healing because God is faithful to restore.

THE STING THAT CUTS DEEP

Few experiences disorient the heart like betrayal. When someone you have poured yourself into suddenly turns their back on you, the pain is layered. You grieve not only what they did, but also who you thought they were. It makes you question your judgment, your kindness, and sometimes even your faith.

I remember one betrayal clearly. A pastor I had known for

years, who I considered a friend, an encourager, and a fellow laborer in ministry, approached me with a manuscript he hoped to publish. Of course, I was glad to help. I own a small publishing company, and even though he could not afford the standard rates, I took on the work myself, providing minor editing, along with the layout and design, so the final book would be something meaningful. And it turned out to be a beautiful, professionally bound book. He was pleased, and I was too.

But everything changed when it came time for distribution. He pressed me for the original digital file, something we never release due to contractual protections. I resisted, but he insisted, and against my better judgment, I gave in. He took that file, went to a third-party printer, and began distributing the book himself. He never paid the agreed-upon royalties. He never compensated me for the extra time and labor I invested. And he never acknowledged the breach of trust.

I reached out and pleaded for integrity, but he denied any wrongdoing. Eventually, he avoided all conversations about it altogether. It was not the financial loss that cut deep; it was the betrayal by someone I had called a friend. I was left with questions any of us would ask after such terrible and unwarranted mistreatment: *Was I blind? Did I miss the signs? Why didn't I see it coming?*

After such a deep betrayal, we often ask God hard questions: *Why would You let this happen? Where were You when the knife went in? Why didn't You protect me?*

I know. I have wrestled with those questions more times than I can count. Over time, I have come to learn that God does not ignore betrayal. He does not overlook injustice. He does not shrug off the heartbreak of someone left holding the shards of a broken friendship.

He sees it all, and He is close by. The very moment you were let down, the second you felt used, discarded, or deceived, He was there holding your heart, even if you could not feel His presence. God does not waste betrayal. He uses it in ways we rarely understand at the time. He uses it to deepen our dependence on Him, to sharpen our discernment, and to gently loosen our grip on people we may have clung to too tightly. Through this, He reminds us that no matter how dear a relationship may be, only Jesus will never fail us.

So, if your heart is heavy today, if someone walked away, or stayed long enough to do harm, know that you are not foolish for trusting, you are not weak for hurting, and you what you have endured matters deeply to God.

Healing begins when you bring every broken piece to the One who still holds your story in His hands.

BIBLICAL EXAMPLES OF BETRAYAL

If you ever find yourself questioning God or your own judgment after being betrayed, the Scriptures offer comfort. Many have felt the sting of betrayal firsthand. And when I think about betrayal in the Bible, I see testimonies that feel heartbreakingly familiar. These are not just stories of people long ago. They are testimonies of hearts, much like ours, left reeling. There is comfort in that, because in their stories, we discover companionship in our suffering.

King David illustrates this pain vividly. When his son Absalom rose up in rebellion, his trusted counselor, Ahithophel, turned against him as well, joining the revolt. David did not just lose an advisor; he lost a beloved friend. His grief is recorded in Psalm 55: *"For it was not an enemy that reproached me; then I could have borne it... But it was thou, a man mine equal, my guide, and mine acquaintance. We took sweet counsel together, and walked unto the house of God in company."*

Ahithophel's betrayal was both political and personal. Once a close confidant who shared meals with David and guided his steps, he now offered his wisdom to the enemy. The wound cut deeper than any sword, yet it foreshadowed something far greater and more costly: the ultimate betrayal of the King of kings, Jesus Christ, who would face treachery at the most critical hour of His life.

Jesus' betrayal came from those closest to Him. Judas, who had walked with Him for several years, shared meals with Him, witnessed the miracles, and was even sent out to minister in Jesus' name, sold Him out for thirty pieces of silver, sealing the betrayal with a kiss. As if that were not enough, Peter, Jesus' boldest disciple, swore that he would never deny his Lord. But that very evening, under fear and pressure, he did precisely that, declaring, *"I know not the man"* (Matthew 26:74).

Jesus knew these wounds of betrayal deeply. He did not merely witness treachery; He bore it. He felt it all, every sting and ache. That is why, when you bring your pain to Him, you are not speaking to a distant God. You are coming to Someone who has been kissed by a traitor and denied by a friend. Someone who knows the sting of betrayal from the inside, who understands the pain, the confusion, the tears.

What takes my breath away isn't just that He endured betrayal and so much suffering, but how He responded. He did not lash out, shut down, or build walls. He offered bread to the betrayer. He restored the denier. He forgave the ones who nailed Him to a cross.

So, when you don't know what to do with your pain, look no

further than Christ's loving example. If David faced betrayal, and Jesus endured it, can we expect to be exempt? Therefore, take comfort: betrayal has always been part of the cost of opening your heart to others.

WHY GOD ALLOWS BETRAYAL

If God truly loves us, why doesn't He stop betrayal before it reaches us? Why does He allow someone we trusted to turn and wound us so deeply? These are valid questions. But Scripture never promises that following Christ will spare us from betrayal. In fact, Jesus said the opposite: *"The servant is not greater than his lord. If they have persecuted me, they will also persecute you"* (John 15:20). Betrayal becomes one of the wounds we share with Christ, yet He faced it first so that we would never have to walk through it alone.

So why does God allow it? Sometimes betrayal reveals what we would never have seen otherwise. It unmasks false loyalty, exposes hidden motives, and brings to light where our trust may have been misplaced. God also uses betrayal to sharpen discernment, deepen dependence, purify faith, loosen our grip on people we leaned on too heavily, and remind us that only Jesus will never fail us.

Sometimes betrayal becomes the turning point that moves us out of places we were never meant to stay. If that person had remained in your life, maybe you would have settled. Perhaps you would have compromised your calling. But God, in His mercy, allowed the rupture to redirect you and to re-center your life on Christ.

So if someone you trusted turned on you, please do not assume, for a moment, that God was absent. Do not believe He overlooked your pain. He saw every word, heard every lie, and felt the wounds you could not bring yourself to articulate. While He may not answer everything now, He promises that none of it is wasted.

God is working through the betrayal. He is shaping you with wisdom, humbling what needs softening, strengthening what is fragile, and forming Christ's likeness within you. That does not mean you will not grieve; it means you can grieve with hope.

THE EMOTIONAL TOLL OF BETRAYAL

Betrayal does not just hurt; it lingers. I remember how it felt after being betrayed by my former pastor friend. We had shared so much. Prayed together. Labored together. So when he turned, it wasn't just the loss of a book project; it was the loss of friendship, dignity, and peace. Perhaps the worst of it was the confusion that followed. I kept asking myself, "How did I misread him? Was I so naïve? Should I have known better?" That's what betrayal does. It shakes your confidence in others *and* yourself.

You begin to question your judgment. Your kindness. Even your worth. The wound suggests, *Maybe this happened because of you.* And if you are not careful, you begin to believe the lie.

I know that voice. It told me to stop helping people. To shut the door of my heart. To be more guarded. Because if I never let anyone in again, no one could hurt me again.

But that kind of protection comes at a cost. Yes, it might keep out the pain, but it also keeps out the healing—the joy of connection, the comfort of friendship, and the beauty of trust restored.

Jesus did not do that. After betrayal, He did not close Himself off, harden, or lash out. He stayed tender. He wept. He prayed. He gave Judas the opportunity to repent, and He welcomed Peter back with grace. And the same Spirit who sustained Him now strengthens us to walk that path, not by our own resolve, but by His power in us.

So, if you are carrying the ache, feeling the weight of someone's betrayal pressing on your soul, let yourself feel it. Cry if you need to. Do not bury the pain and pretend you're fine. Bring it to Jesus in prayer, because He understands. He will not let your heart break without also holding it in His hands.

THE TEMPTATION TO HARDEN YOUR HEART

When you have been betrayed, your heart wants to shut down. It's instinct, like pulling your hand away from a flame. You tell yourself, *Never again.* You shrink your circle, speak less, trust less. And for a while, it feels wise; you think you are safe and strong.

But if left unchecked, that guardedness slowly hardens into bitterness. What began as protection becomes isolation. Suspicion turns into cynicism. Slowly, almost without noticing, you build a fortress to keep out those who might hurt you, yet in doing so, you end up closing yourself off to those God may send to help you heal.

Scripture warns about this drift. Hebrews 12:15 urges us: *"Looking diligently lest any man fail of the grace of God; lest any root of bitterness springing up trouble you, and thereby many be defiled."*

Bitterness never stays small. It spreads. It distorts. And, if we're not careful, it begins to reshape our hearts into something God never intended.

I have felt that pull many times. After I was betrayed, I convinced myself I was done letting people in. I did not want to relive the pain. I did not want to invest in someone else's vision, only to be taken advantage of again. *Why take the risk?* I thought. So, I pulled back. I got quieter and trusted less.

But God did not let me stay there. Because when we wall off our hearts, we begin to close ourselves off from God as well. Bitterness distorts how we see others, and it dulls how we hear Him. Tenderness fades. Joy dwindles. And soon, we are not protecting ourselves; we are starving ourselves.

Hebrews gives another warning: *"Take heed... lest any of you be hardened through the deceitfulness of sin"* (Hebrews 3:12-13). Bitterness is deceptive. It causes us to shut down the parts of us meant to stay alive, open, and responsive to His presence.

And friend, I want more for you than that. Yes, avoiding pain might feel safe. But it also means missing the joy of deep connection, the comfort of shared burdens, and the warmth of godly friendship. Most importantly, it dulls your sensitivity to the gentle stirrings of the Holy Spirit.

God never intended for you to live behind barricades. He desires your healing—your ability to trust again, to love again—with a tender heart resting in the hands of the One who knows exactly how to protect it.

Forgiveness is part of that healing. Not because the one who hurt you deserves it, but because *you* do. You deserve freedom from the weight of resentment. You deserve the peace that comes from releasing what was done to you. No, it's not easy. Some betrayals cut so deeply they feel irreparable. But *with God*, even that is possible to restore.

So do not let your heart grow hard. Let it be shaped, softened, and made more like Christ's. For He, too, was betrayed, and He still chose love.

THE POWER OF FORGIVENESS

Forgiveness is not forgetting what occurred. It is not pretending the betrayal didn't hurt. And it's certainly not excusing the wrong. Forgiveness is a deliberate choice to release someone from the debt they owe you, even when everything in you cries out for repayment. And let's be honest: that kind of forgiveness can feel impossible.

When the pastor I trusted betrayed me—taking the manuscript, disregarding our agreement, and keeping the profits—I felt an anger that startled me. I wanted justice. I wanted the world to know what he had done. But God began to lead me down a different path because what was happening inside me mattered more than the situation itself. So, I chose to forgive, knowing that clinging to the offense would only poison me further. Forgiveness became the way I freed myself from carrying the weight of what he had done. I released the debt and entrusted it to God.

Did it make the pain vanish? No. But it loosened its grip.

Forgiveness does not erase the past, but it does break the chain that drags the past into your future. It's how we lay the offense down at the feet of the only Judge who sees every detail clearly and who promises to set matters right.

On the cross, Jesus perfectly modeled forgiveness. Looking down at the very ones who betrayed, mocked, and crucified Him, He prayed: *"Father, forgive them; for they know not what they do"* (Luke 23:34). In His moment of deepest agony, He still chose mercy.

And that same mercy lives in you because the Spirit of Christ helps you release what you cannot carry. Forgiveness is rarely a one-time act. Some days, you will have to forgive again and again as the memories return and the ache resurfaces. But with each act of forgiveness, your heart grows lighter, your soul breathes a little deeper, and your wound begins to heal.

MOVING FORWARD WITHOUT BITTERNESS

Betrayal leaves a bruise, but bitterness becomes a prison. At first, you think you are simply being cautious, but that caution slowly hardens. You begin to look at people differently. You expect disappointment. You anticipate rejection. And without even realizing it, you start filtering everything through a wound that never had a chance to heal.

That is what bitterness does, it begins to affect how you see everyone. After I was betrayed, I noticed that shift in myself. I grew skeptical and withdrawn. I second-guessed people's motives even when they meant well. I told myself I was just being discerning, but deep down, I began to recognize that bitterness had settled in.

The problem with bitterness is that it bleeds into your relationships, your decisions, and even your prayers. A wound left untreated festers. That is why forgiveness, while essential, is not the end of the journey. We must also move forward by refusing to let the betrayal define who we become. God never asks us to deny reality; He asks us to trust Him with the outcome.

Bitterness wants to keep you stuck, but God wants to lead you into a life not ruled by what they did, but by what He is doing. Moving forward means surrendering the role of judge. It means saying, "Lord, You saw it. I don't have to hold onto this any longer. I release it into Your hands."

That does not mean you will suddenly feel light and happy overnight. Healing rarely works that way. Some days you will grieve. Some moments you will sting. But every time you choose grace over resentment, your heart becomes a little more whole.

And know that not everyone who betrays you walks away proud. Some leave the situation haunted, privately convicted by their own conscience. But even that must be entrusted to God. You are not responsible for their journey, only for your response. And in the long run, that is far lighter to deal with.

The alternative is to live open-hearted again. Let God bring the right people in His timing. Learn from the pain, but do not live in it. Be honest about the wound, but do not make it your identity. And if restoration ever comes, thank Him. If it does not, trust Him.

Moving forward does not mean forgetting; it means refusing to stay stuck in the past. You are not what others did to you. You belong to God, walking forward in grace, with your eyes on Jesus, not on the wound, but on the healing He is bringing.

GOD SEES GOD KNOWS GOD WILL MAKE IT RIGHT

One of the sharpest aches of betrayal is watching the person who hurt you move on as if nothing happened. They walk away, smile in photos, begin new chapters, and seem to thrive while you are still trying to catch your breath in the wreckage.

If you are not careful, that sense of injustice can start to eat away at your peace. But here is what steadies me: God sees. God knows. God will make it right. He knows the whole story—every detail, every wound, every word spoken behind closed doors. As

Romans 12:19 reminds us, *"Vengeance is mine; I will repay, saith the Lord."*

That is a promise of protection. It means justice belongs to God and not to you. You do not have to carry the burden of proving your innocence or demanding your side of the story be heard. Your Father in Heaven already knows it, and He cares.

You are not crying into the void. You are not fighting a losing battle. You are not forgotten. You are held by a God who is merciful *and* who knows how to convict hearts, expose truth, protect His children, and deal rightly with all matters in His timing.

Jesus understands this better than anyone. He wasn't just betrayed by Judas. He was rejected by the very people He came to save. Abandoned in His darkest hour. Falsely accused. Mocked. Beaten. Silenced.

And how did He respond? He did not retaliate. He did not curse them. He did not demand justice on the spot. Instead, Peter tells us, *"Who when he was reviled, reviled not again; when he suffered, he threatened not; but committed himself to him that judgeth righteously"* (1 Peter 2:23). That's the example He left for us: entrusting Himself to the Father who judges rightly and makes all things whole in His time.

Sometimes, God's justice shows up through repentance and restoration. Other times, He reveals it through separation, removing people from your life to spare you deeper harm. And occasionally, His justice looks like letting go without ever getting the apology you deserved... and still choosing peace.

That's not giving up. That's growing up in faith. One day, every betrayal will be accounted for. Every tear you have cried in secret is seen by the One who bottles them and records them in His book (Psalm 56:8). Nothing is overlooked by God. No wrong is forgotten. And no injustice escapes His holy attention.

So, take a breath. You do not have to chase resolution. You do not have to explain yourself anymore. Just stay faithful. God is watching. God is working. And yes, He will make it right.

A FINAL WORD TO THE WOUNDED

Betrayal leaves a wound, but it need not leave a wall. It's tempting, I know. After someone's broken your trust, opening up again feels like the last thing you ever want to do. But what if that wound could become more than a scar? What if it could become a testimony?

The devil wants your betrayal to define you. He wants it to sour your spirit, isolate your heart, and convince you it is safer to live guarded and bitter than open and healed. But Jesus longs to redeem it, taking what was meant for harm and turning it into healing for you and for others. In 2 Corinthians 1:4, we are told that *"[God] comforteth us in all our tribulation, that we may be able to comfort them which are in any trouble."*

That's not merely a sweet verse for sympathy cards. It is a picture of redemption. Your pain, when surrendered, can become someone else's rescue. Maybe you've already seen this in your life. Perhaps you've sat across from someone walking a road you once stumbled down, and you knew what to say because you had lived it yourself.

That is the beauty of God's healing. He does not just mend you; He sends you. He uses your scars as invitations. He turns your pain into a platform where grace can be seen. And you do not need a spotlight, a pulpit, eloquence, or credentials. You only need a story that's honest, surrendered, and real.

So do not hide the wound. Let it speak of the God who stayed, the Saviour who understands, and the Spirit who gave you the strength to stand again. Your betrayal is not the end of your story. It might just be the beginning of someone else's healing.

———— **11** ————

LONELINESS:
ALONE IN THE CROWD

Loneliness is one of those wounds we rarely talk about. It does not show up on prayer lists. It does not get preached about much. But it's everywhere: sitting in pews, waiting in checkout lines, and riding home after a long day's work.

We smile when greeting coworkers, nod along in conversations, and post happy pictures online. But beneath all the politeness, small talk, and daily routines, many of us are carrying a heavy ache that is not always obvious. It is not just sadness, nor is it stress. It is something quieter and emptier: loneliness. And it is more common than we think.

Loneliness is not only for the elderly or the forgotten. It does not belong just to the shy or the new visitor sitting quietly in the back row of the church. It hides in the hearts of pastors, missionaries, spouses, parents, teenagers, people you admire, and even someone sitting right beside you. It wears nice clothing, tracks calories, fills calendars, and sometimes says all the right words. But behind the mask lie the doubts and questions: *Does anyone really know me? Would anyone notice if I disappeared?*

Maybe you've felt it, too. Perhaps you tried to speak up once, only to be met with clichés or shallow comforts: *"Just pray more. Get plugged in. God is enough."* And while those words were well-intended, they were not helpful because you were not looking for a pat answer; you were longing to be seen.

Loneliness does not just visit you when you are by yourself. It follows you to church, sneaks behind you into your home, and slips into your busy days and quiet evenings. It rides with you in the car, hovers while you run errands, and whispers in the noise of a crowded room. It shows up even in the good moments, when everything looks fine on the outside, but your heart knows something is missing.

Have you ever felt a sudden wave of emptiness wash over you, even in a crowded room or at a happy celebration? Everyone is laughing, the music's playing, and yet, something inside aches. I've known that sense of loneliness, too. Friendships that faded without explanation. Conversations that skimmed the surface. Seasons of giving everything, only to go home with nothing. Over the years, I have come to understand that this sense of loneliness is actually the soul's yearning to be closer to God. We were made for Him, and no matter how full our lives appear—how rich, powerful, or surrounded by people and entertainment—there remains a quiet space only He can fill.

The ache we sometimes call loneliness may be a much-needed reminder: nothing in this world can satisfy what was created to be fulfilled by God alone. I've discovered that when placed in His hands, loneliness can become sacred ground, as the silence makes space to hear what you didn't realize you needed: *You are not overlooked. You are not forgotten.*

WHEN THE BOND QUIETLY BREAKS

It is strange how a friendship can unravel without warning. One day, everything feels normal. You're texting, laughing, sharing life. And then something shifts. Maybe it's not a fight or a big fallout; it is distance and a slow drift you cannot explain.

Sometimes I still think about people who were once a deep part of my life. People whose company I enjoyed, prayed with, and shared burdens and dreams with. Folks who talked about the future as if it were ours to walk through together. But something changed in one particular relationship, and I still do not fully know why. There was no argument or betrayal. No falling-out worth mentioning. Just… silence. He stopped reaching out. Or maybe I did. Either way, the connection faded. It did not die in a fire; it died in a drought, simply because no one remembered to keep watering the relationship.

That kind of loss comes without closure, but it brings confusion. You wonder if you said something wrong, if you were too much, or maybe not enough. You scroll through old messages, asking yourself: "Was this the moment it all changed?" You try to move on. But something still tugs at your heart.

Sometimes God places people into our lives for only a brief moment, and yet that moment changes everything. Take David and the prophet Samuel, for example. Samuel appeared when David was still a shepherd boy, just long enough to anoint him as king and declare God's calling over his life. Afterward, Scripture never records them crossing paths again. David didn't even attend Samuel's funeral. Yet that short encounter shaped the course of his life forever. God often uses brief friendships in the same way: even fleeting connections can leave a lasting mark on our hearts and direct us toward our purpose.

Other times, friendships don't just fade; they are intentionally redirected by God because we've grown too comfortable leaning on them rather than on God.

Later in David's life, we see this with King Achish of the Philistines. David had built an unusual friendship with Achish, even finding a place of refuge in enemy territory. It wasn't ideal, but it worked—until it didn't. Sixteen months later, the Philistine leaders rejected David's involvement in battle. And even though David protested, *"But what have I done?"* (1 Samuel 29:8), he was sent away. Achish had no problem with him, but God did because David no longer belonged there. He was not called to fight alongside the Philistines. He was called to trust God, even when the path was more challenging.

So, David and his men left that friendship behind and returned to Israel. It was a harder place, yes, but it called them to depend fully on the one true God. Sometimes, when the friendship fades, it is not rejection but God redirecting us to lean a little less on people, and a lot more on Him.

One of the most painful aspects of losing friendships is seeing them move on with their lives while your life feels paused in grief. Their absence can sometimes stir those familiar pangs of loneliness within us.

I've wrestled with that void too. In my first week of college, I quickly formed a close friendship with someone who felt like a spiritual brother, a true gift from God. Decades later, I shared some concerns about a project he was involved in. Maybe I was too direct, or maybe my words hit a tender spot. But afterward, all I got was silence. He never responded. Never called. Never explained. Twenty-five years of friendship *gone*.

Then there was another friend, one I had known for over ten years. I once shared a real-life story that involved her in one of my blog posts, while remaining discreet and respectful. She recognized herself in it. Instead of reaching out or asking for clarity, she assumed the worst. She sent me a text, and that was it. No conversation. No grace. Just a final word and a locked door. Ten years of shared history, gone in a moment.

These are not just small disappointments. They are deep, disorienting losses. When someone walks away like that, you lose more than their presence, you lose the comfort of being known by them, the intimate conversations, the rapport, and the understanding. Perhaps the worst part is never getting the chance to make it right. You are left with a wound where a friendship once was, and the ache of having been known, only to feel discarded.

In that place, the questions come fast and sharp: *Did I say too much? Am I that easy to walk away from? Was I only valuable when I stayed quiet?*

But here's what I have learned in the wake of silence: people may disappear without a word, but God never walks out. In their absence, His presence remains. He heals in ways that don't demand attention. He does not always fill the space with answers, but He fills it with His comforting Self. In time, you realize what you needed most was a reminder: *"You're still Mine. You are beloved."*

If someone's absence still lingers in your chest, if you catch yourself wondering what you could have done differently: God did not leave when they did. He stayed. And in time, His presence comforts the silence in a way their words never could.

LONELINESS IS MORE THAN BEING ALONE

There is a kind of loneliness that does not look like loneliness at all. On the outside, your life might seem full. You have a family, a church community, and a packed schedule. You serve, lead, and smile. Yet deep inside, you feel you are quietly vanishing into someone no one really sees. This is the kind of sorrow that most people do not talk about, especially those who are busy and needed, because it is hard to explain feeling hollow and exhausted when everything in your life looks fine. It is hard even to call it loneliness (though it is) when people in your life are thanking you for your help, complimenting your kindness, or counting on you to show up, all while you are slowly withering inside.

I have lived in that space most of my life. I have gone to lunch with friends, sat through Bible studies, and chatted after work, all while feeling invisible. That feeling has stayed with me, not because anyone was unkind, but because no one really knew the version of me that was tired, confused, and emotionally threadbare. The real me hid behind the polite smile, and no one noticed.

And I have heard this same inner agony from others, too. Single mothers surrounded by children who need them every second, yet inside, they feel deafeningly alone. They are never off duty, always important, but rarely known. What they long for is not necessarily more help, but connection: a space where they are seen as more than a provider or protector, but as a person.

This kind of loneliness wears you down subtly, day after day. What makes it worse is that you often do not know how to put it into words. How do you say, "I feel invisible," when everyone keeps telling you how much they appreciate you?

There is a story in John 5 about a man by the pool of Bethesda that has stayed with me for a long time. For thirty-eight years, he lay beside the steps, waiting for healing. Day after day, he watched others descend into the water and rise again, whole and restored. But no one ever stopped to help him. He waited year after weary year like a shadow no one noticed.

Can you imagine watching people come and go—many finding healing, others moving on—while you stay stuck? Eventually, you stop hoping anyone will come or even see you. That is what loneliness can do. It lies, telling you, "You don't matter." It convinces you that your moment has passed, that healing is for everyone else, and that maybe even God has moved on without you.

But the story does not end there. Jesus shows up. He does not walk past. He stops. He sees the man. And He asks a question that reaches deeper than any surface need: *"Wilt thou be made whole?"*

In that moment, Jesus was reaching not for the man's exterior wound, but for something deeper: his wounded soul. Yes, he was paralyzed, but worse, he was alone, isolated, and discarded. And in that moment, Jesus offered him more than movement. He provided restoration for his body and his sense of worth.

I am convinced Jesus still does this. He walks into unseen places. He sees the mother, tears in her eyes, folding laundry. He sees the pastor who's poured himself dry. He sees the one scrolling through their phone at midnight, wondering why no one checks in. When He asks, "Do you want to be whole?" — He is offering belonging, intimacy, and wholeness.

That ache you feel is not a flaw. It is not proof that you are broken beyond repair. It is a signal, a cry for something more than applause or productivity. It is the hunger to be fully known… and still loved.

And the good news is that Jesus does not wait for you to fix it. He draws near. He crosses the distance. And He affirms what your heart has needed to hear all along: "I see you. You are not invisible to Me."

WHEN LONELINESS
REVEALS SOMETHING DEEPER

Loneliness rarely gives warning signs in advance. Sometimes it follows a loss: a friend who walked away, a relationship that faded, or a move to a place where no one knows your name. Or maybe, one day, after a long series of inner or external battles, you wake up and the heaviness is simply there. You go through the motions, but inside, something feels hollow, and you cannot explain why.

For a long time, I used to ask, *Where is this coming from?* But over the years, I have learned to ask a different question: *Lord, what are You trying to show me through this?* I do this because loneliness is rarely just an emotion; it is a mirror. It reveals what we have ignored, reflecting buried wounds and hidden dependencies. And if we stop running from it, it may point us not only to brokenness around us but to the unfinished healing within us.

Sometimes the real disconnect is not horizontal; it is vertical. I was not lonely because someone left me; I was lonely because somewhere along the way, I had drifted from God. This wasn't an open rebellion, but more so took the appearance of busyness, distraction, and burnout. I was still in ministry, still helping others, still outwardly "present." But inside, I was far from Him. And the farther I drifted, the lonelier I became, even in a crowded room.

Sin can do that, showing up in subtle compromises, like grudges we won't release, pride that pushes us to perform, and envy hidden beneath a polite smile. They do not feel like rebellion, yet they rob us of intimacy with God. When His closeness fades, everything else begins to unravel.

That's why some sadness is both emotional *and* spiritual. It is the pang of being out of rhythm with the One who created us. When that kind of loneliness settles in, it can feel all-consuming. It makes you question your worth, your purpose, and even your place in God's heart. Yet often God allows that pang to remain, not to punish us, but to draw us home.

But not every lonely season is caused by sin. Sometimes it is simply fatigue: the slow erosion of passion, the heaviness of routines that no longer stir your heart, or the longing of a dream that did not come to pass. Nothing is catastrophically wrong, yet everything feels muted. The joy is gone. The fire has dimmed. And you wonder, *What now?*

When loneliness stretches on for a significant amount of time, it can start to convince you that nothing matters, that joy may never return, and that this emptiness is your new normal. Sometimes, these whispers edge into depression, pressing in with a weight that makes the days longer and burdens the heart. Yet even in that space, God is not absent. Often, I have discovered that the drying up of old wells, so to speak, is His way of leading us toward something deeper: real sustenance and intimacy that come only from Him. Here loneliness can become holy ground, clearing away the clutter, stripping illusions, and creating space for honesty and a renewed dependence on God.

So, if you find yourself there right now, know that your loneliness is not proof that God has left you. More often than not, it is His invitation to draw you closer than you have been in a long time. And if you walk through it, you will find that loneliness was meant to lead you to the presence of the One who will never walk away.

THE SILENCE THAT ECHOES

Not every loss is loud. Sometimes, it comes softly, almost like a slow burn. You might feel it when no one notices you leaving the room, or when your birthday passes without a card or any acknowledgment. Maybe calls go unanswered, the texts remain unread, and an empty cavern forms where your friendship once stood. You feel like the only one who cares, ruminating over what may or may not have happened between the two of you. In that ache, you begin to wonder whether the path you walked together was ever real.

At first, you grieve the person. But over time, it is not just their absence that hurts; it's what their absence reshaped in you. Their silence unsettled how you trust. Their disappearance made you question your worth. *Was I too much? Not enough? Too inconvenient?*

One of the sharpest pangs (deep in my heart, and maybe in yours, too) is not only the sense of being shut out, but the pain of knowing you were left out. Especially when the very people who should have embraced you choose distance instead. That kind of wound lingers, splitting the heart apart.

Friendship was never meant to be disposable. We were created for bonds that endure. So when someone vanishes without explanation, a wound remains that logic cannot mend. And without closure, that wound can fester into questions that reverberate long after they are gone. You rarely talk about it because it seems like no one else would understand. Everyone else seems to have "their people." But you have grown cautious. You are still cordial, but your walls are a little higher because once someone disappears without warning, it changes the way you let others in.

Sometimes you even rehearse imaginary conversations where you finally say what you never could. Where they listen. Where they stay. But those are only dreams. You wake and they are still gone.

That is the part people often overlook about loneliness: the burden of carrying unfinished stories. The apology you never got to give. The misunderstanding you could not mend. The tension that never softened. And yes, the nagging ache of wondering if it might have been different... if you had handled it better. And if you are not careful, those silent goodbyes can twist into lies: *Maybe I'm not worth staying for. Maybe I'm too complicated. Perhaps something is wrong with me.*

Loneliness touches everyone, even the Apostle Paul. He admitted, *"At my first answer no man stood with me, but all men forsook me"* (2 Timothy 4:16). Sometimes the most faithful servants of God stand alone, misunderstood, unsupported, and unseen. However, Paul did not stay in despair. He reminded himself, *"Notwithstanding the Lord stood with me, and strengthened me"* (v. 17). When others walked away, Paul did not question his worth; he anchored it in the One who remained.

That same truth has carried me through blurred tears, unanswered texts, and friends who left without a goodbye. God does not measure your worth by who stayed. He does not define you by the silence others left behind. Sometimes He allows those open-ended stories to reveal how fragile our foundations were, and to shift our weight back to Him gently. He may not resolve every lingering question, but He gives us something far better than closure: His unshakable presence. A nearness that steadies what explanations never could.

THE PURPOSE IN THE PAIN

Loneliness has a way of making you reach for anything that quiets the ache: distractions, numbing habits, or surface relationships that fill your calendar but never touch your heart. In those moments, what you reach for shapes who you are becoming. You can numb yourself, or you can lean into the stillness of God and the unhurried presence of a Father who does not ask you to perform.

For years, I saw loneliness only as something to escape—a numbness to pray away so life could get back to feeling good again. But over time, I have come to understand that there are places in the soul God can touch only when no one else is around. Loneliness brings you face-to-face with yourself. Not the version you present to others, but the one who is trying to feel "enough." It reveals how easily we can feel like we do not measure up, how we pour ourselves out for others and still feel unseen, and how quickly we start believing our worth depends on getting everything right.

These realizations expose the hidden places where our identity has been tethered to being liked, needed, praised, or included. And when those ties fall away, it does not feel like growth; it feels like coming undone. But in God's hands, even that place becomes sacred, because it leads us toward healing rather than away from it.

In one of my loneliest seasons, I realized I was doing many things *for* God but very few *with* Him. I had the motions down: busy hands, a full schedule, and prayers mumbled between obligations. But my soul was starving for communion. Loneliness exposed that gap, and in its quiet way, it drew me closer to Him.

It is in this surrendered space that loneliness can become a classroom of sorts, where God teaches us to stop performing and start resting. Where we learn to bring Him our unpolished prayers (the clumsy, teary, and yes, the silent ones). Where we slow down long enough to hear Him whisper what applause and activity never could: *"I still love you. I still see you. Even here."*

And from that place, compassion begins to grow. Once you have felt the sting of isolation, you begin to notice it in others. You move more slowly through a room. You hear what others overlook. You stop needing to impress and start learning how to be present. That is Christ at work in you.

Some of the richest treasures in my life were born in seasons I once begged God to take away. I wrote books I never planned to write, developed empathy I did not know possible, gained a clearer sense of what matters, and uncovered deeper satisfaction with God. I have come to realize loneliness is not punishment; it is preparation for a deeper walk with God.

Sometimes, He allows the crowd to fade so you can learn how to walk with Him when no one else shows up, to form something in you that could not be shaped any other way.

This truth is echoed in Scripture: *"Every branch that beareth fruit, he purgeth it, that it may bring forth more fruit"* (John 15:2). I used to think that pruning referred only to cutting away sin. But sometimes God prunes good things like friendships, routines, and long-cherished dreams. And though it hurts, what He grows in the emptiness often lasts longer than what we lost.

So, if you are feeling hollow, cut off, and forgotten right now, please know that God is not wasting this. He is not absent. He is not punishing you. He is preparing you. And the roots He's growing in this quiet season may reach deeper than you ever imagined. Sometimes the ache we try so hard to escape becomes the very doorway into communion with Him.

And it is often in that doorway—raw, quiet, and unguarded—that something deeper begins to awaken.

Sometimes it is in the moments when you feel emptied out and unsure of what's left that God begins to shift your vision. The supports you once leaned on lose their grip, and suddenly the only foundation holding you up is Christ. In loneliness, you begin to see what truly matters. Not the approval of others, not material stability, not the routines you once clung to, but the steady presence of the living God.

I've learned that these are the moments when God is doing a work no one else can see. He is preparing you, even when it feels like nothing is happening. So don't give up. Do not despise the silence. Do not run from the stillness. Sit with it for a moment longer than feels comfortable, because something good is unfolding right there.

When it feels like everyone has left you... when friends don't understand... when your heart whispers, "Lord, I don't know how much more I can take," that's often where His strength meets you. Not in a loud breakthrough, but in a steadiness that slowly rises within you. And that is when peace comes and you sense Him more clearly, not because the emptiness lifted, but because your eyes finally lifted to the One who walks through it with you.

YOU ARE NOT ALONE

I do not know what shape your loneliness has taken. Maybe it's the empty space beside you at night, the silence in your inbox when no one replies, or the dull pang of being misunderstood even after explaining yourself again and again. I won't pretend there is a quick fix to make the pain vanish. But I can tell you this with absolute certainty: you are not forgotten by the One who formed you and who loves you dearly. Even if no one checks in, even if people walk away without explanation, He has not and He never will.

You are not a project or a burden to God. You do not weary Him with your sadness or disqualify yourself with your silence. You do not have to perform or punish yourself to win back His affection. He already holds you, yes, here and now, even if all you can manage is to sit before Him wordless and weary.

Maybe the silence has grown heavy. Maybe the unanswered questions have thinned your hope. But even there, God is leaning close with comfort: *"You don't have to earn My attention. I see you. I have always seen you. And you are My beloved."*

I understand that it may not feel like enough in the moment. We were made for connection with someone who chooses us, listens, and stays. It is okay to pray for that. Keep asking. God is more than able to bring divine appointments, healing conversations, and unexpected friendships into your journey. I have watched Him do it for me when I had stopped expecting it.

But while you wait, do not let loneliness rewrite your worth. Do not let it convince you that you are broken beyond repair. Because through unanswered texts and endless nights, God was anchoring my identity, not in who accepted me, but in Who created me. He was softening my heart to see others more tenderly and shaping me into the kind of safe place I had always wished someone would be for me.

That does not make loneliness pleasant. But it does make it purposeful. If you are feeling unseen, overlooked, or forgotten, please hear this: it does not mean something is wrong with you. You are not weak. You are growing, more so than you realize. Most of all, you are not alone. Not now. Not ever.

12

DEPRESSION:
THE ACHE OF NOTHINGNESS

Of all the kinds of suffering, depression feels the most personal because it is one of the most invisible torments haunting the human soul. It does not just hurt; it hollows. It does not just ache; it numbs. It wraps itself around grief, betrayal, illness, and fear like a suffocating darkness, distorting everything in sight. It drains strength. It steals the will to try. It convinces you, sometimes in a room full of people, that your very existence is a burden.

Depression is not simple weariness or passing loneliness. It a dark emptiness beneath everything: the absence of hope, the slow fading of life into *nothingness*. Depression feels like falling into an open tomb that is suddenly sealed shut—alive inside, unable to free yourself.

That is why I believe nearly every form of suffering, if left untended, can eventually slip into a form of depression. Many of us know that descent well: the heaviness in the chest that no sleep can cure, the blankness behind the practiced smile, and the pain of feeling invisible even when surrounded by love. I have felt it, and I know how difficult it is to find one's way back.

I have endured long stretches of emotional emptiness and spiritual silence where joy felt unreachable and God felt far away. Some lasted weeks, and others came in brief, unrelenting waves. But one episode stands out to me because of what God revealed in it. In that disorienting encounter in depression, He placed treasures in my heart I could not have found anywhere else that have steadied me ever since.

That is why I do not write these words as a lecturer from a safe distance, but as a companion on the road. I want to sit with you in this, not preach at you. When depression presses in, you often do not need solutions. Sometimes, you just need presence from someone who understands, who will not rush you, and who can gently remind you: You are not losing it. You are not forgotten. And you are not alone.

WHEN THE WEIGHT WON'T LIFT

Depression does not always begin with a tragedy. Sometimes it starts on an ordinary day, with sunlight spilling across the yard, plans unfolding as usual, and nothing outwardly wrong. And then, without warning, the dark cloud comes.

That's what happened to me. I was back in Ohio, visiting family, doing something as simple as walking out of the library with my mother. Nothing had triggered it. Nothing had gone wrong. But suddenly, something inside me gave way. I wasn't sad. I was not stressed. I felt like I was vanishing, as if my soul was falling into a void I could not stop. "Mother," I said, my voice shaky and unfamiliar, "I need to get to the car." How do you explain becoming *nothing*?

That is the nature of depression. It can barge in and rearrange everything, including your thoughts, your energy, your memory, and your ability to care. One moment you are fine. Next, you are wondering if you'll ever find yourself again.

For years, I did not know how to talk about it. Depression felt like a weakness I was not supposed to admit, especially as someone in ministry. People expect strength, optimism, and confident expressions of faith. But what do you do when the faith is still there, yet you feel like you are fading anyway? When you believe God is good... but your emotions are numb, your energy is gone, and even getting dressed in the morning feels like a mountain too high?

Here is what I wish someone had told me years ago: feeling broken does not mean you are worthless. Struggling does not make you a disappointment to God. You are not a failure. And no matter how empty you feel, you are not alone.

Depression can be chronic, and sometimes it stems from a chemical imbalance in the brain and body. But there is a temporary kind that feels anything but temporary when it strikes, and it has many faces. Sometimes it is born of trauma, sometimes of loss, and sometimes of our own sinful choices. And sometimes... it is simply a heavy haze with no apparent cause. However it arrives, it always brings with it the same cruel lie: *You're alone in this. And you should be able to snap out of it.*

I have walked through that murk more times than I can count. I have sat in the void staring into nothing, convinced I might never find my way back. But I am here now, and I am grateful to be able to tell you that there is a way through. I do not have easy answers. But I do have my own story and what I have seen in the wilderness. I know the God who sits with us in the silent void. So let me share a little of my journey and a whole lot of God's Word, and perhaps in the process, you will find yourself less alone in the place you are walking.

THE HAZE THAT DOESN'T LIFT

I remember sitting in the front seat of the car, staring blankly through the windshield while my mother kept asking what was wrong. I did not know how to answer. All I could manage was, "I'm becoming nothingness." Strange words, maybe, to someone who's never been there, but they were the truest ones I had. I felt myself slipping away from the inside out, falling into a void I could not fight.

Depression often feels like a sense of detachment. Things lose their vibrance. Moments lose their meaning. You are alive, but you are not really living. You go through the motions, say what is expected, even smile when needed, but behind your eyes, there is a heavy silence no one else can hear. And most often, you say nothing because you cannot. You lose the words. You lose the strength. Even the will to explain what you cannot understand disappears.

It is tormenting because you feel like a ghost in your own life: surrounded yet unreachable; exhausted yet unable to rest; present but not truly there. The pain is not only emotional; it is also mental, spiritual, and even physical. Then comes the guilt for not being okay, for not having a "medical" reason (even though, in many cases, it is a legitimate health condition), and for loving God, yet still feeling this way.

One of depression's cruelest lies is that your struggle makes you weak, ungrateful, unspiritual, and beyond help. The deeper the depression goes, and the longer it is left unspoken, the more it numbs you until you feel nonexistent, almost like you have disappeared inside your own body.

But I am grateful to have learned that depression is not a failure of faith. It is a form of suffering that Scripture understands intimately. After the greatest revival of his ministry, the prophet Jonah spiraled into despair—angry, isolated, and begging God to end his life. King Hezekiah, crushed by a terminal diagnosis, turned his face to the wall and wept bitterly. Jeremiah, overwhelmed by mockery and rejection, cursed the day he was born and wished he had never existed. And Hannah, aching for what her heart longed for most, wept before the Lord with such anguish she couldn't form words. These were chosen vessels of God. And yet, each of them knew despair that nearly broke them.

So, if you have ever thought, *"Real Christians shouldn't feel this way,"* let me lovingly tell you: that is not true. Some of the people God used in remarkable ways, at one time, fell into their own bottomless, dark pit of despair.

If you are in that pit today, you are not disqualified or abandoned. God has not turned His face away. He has not given up on you. Even if all you can do is whisper Christ's name, He hears you. He is still with you. And He is not going anywhere.

WHEN OBEDIENCE BREAKS THE HAZE

That day in Ohio, when I felt like I was slipping into "nothingness," I did not want to move. I sat in the passenger seat, staring off in the distance, the dark cloud of depression pressing in heavier with each passing second. Eventually, I prayed, only mustering up the words, "God... free me."

And then came a knock. A woman stood outside the window, shivering in the cold. Her car had broken down beside us, and she needed help. The truth is, I did not want to help her; I could not even help myself. Yet in that moment, I sensed a gentle nudge from the Holy Spirit. *Help her.*

Everything in me wanted to stay frozen, but somehow, I opened the door and stepped out. My legs felt like lead. My mind was foggy. I could hardly string words together. She ended up connecting the cables while I stood there, numb, awkward, and unsure.

And then another gentle nudge came: *Share Christ with her.* I hesitated. My voice was weak. My thoughts were empty. But I knew I had to try. "Can I ask you something?" I said softly.

She looked up.

"Could I share something with you that matters even more than your car: salvation through Jesus Christ?"

To my surprise, she said yes. I stumbled through the first few sentences, halting and unsure. Then something shifted. The haze didn't vanish all at once, but it began to lift. My thoughts found footing. My voice steadied, and the words came easier. As I spoke about Christ, the depression that had felt suffocating just moments earlier began to loosen its grip. The cold air no longer mattered. My heart, vacant only minutes before, was suddenly burning with something alive and holy.

I have never forgotten that moment. It taught me that obedience, even in weakness, still holds power. Healing does not always come when you *feel* better. Sometimes it begins when you stop waiting to feel better and simply respond obediently, whether that is stepping out of the car, as I did, or whispering a prayer for help, even if your lips tremble. Now, this does not mean depression disappears in an instant. But it does mean it does not get the final word.

The smallest act of faith can crack open space for God's light to enter. And sometimes, in helping someone else, you discover God was helping you all along.

WHEN THE SOUL WANDERS

Sometimes depression settles in, and its cause is unclear. Other times, if you are honest, you know the reason, it is rooted in the spiritual. It might be the lonely ache of a heart that has drifted from its Source. The soul was never meant to live far from God. So, when it does, something inside begins to unravel. Joy fades and peace erodes. In its place, a dull sadness grows.

I have had seasons when I opened my Bible and could not absorb a single word. There were times when I went through all the motions, but deep down, my heart was numb. Then one day, I woke up and wondered why everything felt so heavy, why the vibrance of life had faded, why God felt so distant.

It is not always sin that leads to depression, but sometimes sin feeds the silence. In my own past, I recall times I've had a covetous desire I refused to release, an attitude I justified, and a bitterness I nurtured because it made me feel vindicated. But none of that was good for me or made me secure. It made me numb and became fertile ground for despair.

God does not stop loving us when we wander. When we stop listening to Him, the distance we have created feels like abandonment, as if He's gone and does not care.

However, silence is not always punishment. Sometimes it is an invitation from God, saying, "Come back," with the tender reach of a Father calling His child home. And in that moment, you realize that sometimes depression is simply a reminder that your soul is homesick.

Depression may feel like a brick wall. But often it is a doorway where God meets you, inviting you into one small step, one quiet confession, one honest prayer. And the moment you turn back toward Him, the distance begins to close.

WHEN YOU QUESTION WHO YOU ARE

Have you ever looked in the mirror and thought, *"I don't even know who I am anymore"*?

Maybe you cannot explain what changed, but you know that something inside feels missing. That is what depression does. It makes you feel sad, small, and empty, like a hollow shell. It tries to convince you that your best days are over and that God has moved on and lost track of you.

I recall those moments, standing in the ruins of myself, unsure if I'd ever find my way back again. The prophet Jeremiah knew that place, too. In Jeremiah 20, we see a weary prophet in the service of God, emotionally frayed, spiritually exhausted, and pushed beyond his limits. His words are raw and filled with anguish: *"O LORD, thou hast deceived me... I am in derision daily... cursed be the day wherein I was born."*

He did not feel holy or brave; he felt erased. But here is where grace intercedes: God never rebuked or scolded His prophet for collapsing under the weight. Instead, He let those cries remain in

Scripture. He preserved them so you and I would know that He can handle our collapse.

God did not thunder back, *"Get it together, prophet."* No, He stayed near. I find it encouraging that God chose to keep Jeremiah's breakdown in the Bible. If Jeremiah's grief was worth recording, then your grief is not beyond God's compassion. Why? Because God knew we would need it. He knew there would be days when you'd forget who you are, when your heart would murmur, *You're not useful anymore. You're not strong enough. You're not worthy to be called His.*

And on those days, He wanted you to remember Jeremiah. Not the preacher, but the man curled up in sorrow, questioning everything... and still held by God.

Your identity is not measured by how "together" you are. It is not determined by how inspired you feel or how productive you are. Your identity is rooted in Christ Jesus, and He never forgets you. Not in your confusion. Not in your numbness, and not even when your prayers come out as silence. So, if all you can whisper today is, "Are You still there, Lord?" — that's enough.

Even prophets collapsed, and the faithful broke. But that does not change how God sees you. He is not ashamed of your ache, nor is He surprised by your breakdown. He is still writing your story. Even in the place where you've forgotten your name. God has not.

WHEN SUFFERING RESHAPES YOU

I would not have chosen depression or signed up for the loneliness that cuts like an invisible knife. But if I am honest, some of the deepest, most lasting work God has ever done in me came through those very seasons.

Pain slows you down and softens your edges. It teaches you to feel what others feel, even when they do not have the words to describe it. Depression has made me more compassionate and more attuned to suffering that hides beneath the surface. Before, I could preach to pain, but now I can sit with it.

That's the unique gift of suffering: it can refine us, humble us, and equip us. God never wastes the wilderness. He uses it to chisel into us virtues that comfort never could.

Scripture speaks to this hidden work. Job 12:22 says, *"He discovereth deep things out of darkness, and bringeth out to light the shadow of death."*

In seasons of darkness, God has a way of uncovering what comfort has kept hidden. He uses those very seasons to expose what could not be seen in ease, revealing truths about our hearts, our lives, and even Himself. What feels like darkness to us often becomes the place where God brings hidden things into the light, matters that must be seen.

When God does this deep, unseen work, it inevitably changes the way we carry ourselves in the world. Something truer and more grounded begins to take shape. You no longer speak *about* pain, you recognize it, because you have lived with it.

We often assume leadership is born of strength and charisma; however, the wisest leaders I have known are those who have bled much. People who have walked through depression: who have lost pieces of themselves they never got back, and emerged with empathy, humility, and prayers of intimate depth.

When you have been stripped bare by suffering, you stop leading from image and start leading from surrender. You stop trying to impress and start learning to serve. You stop assuming and start truly seeing.

Depression has deepened my ministry, transforming the way I pray, speak, and write. It smoothed out the sharp edges of my theology and gave it a heartbeat. I do not celebrate the seasons of depression, but I no longer curse them either. Because through them, God carved out parts of me I did not know needed reshaping. And maybe, that's part of what He is doing in you, too.

WHEN JOY FEELS FAR AWAY

We often wish healing from depression would come quickly. That after one heartfelt prayer, or one hymn, or one tearful conversation, everything would snap back into place. But that is rarely how it works.

Sometimes joy returns slowly. It might be in the choice to get out of bed when staying under the covers feels easier. It could be in the opening of your Bible and reading a chapter, even if it feels distant. Perhaps it is in a short, honest prayer spoken from a weary heart. It is most certainly in reaching out to a person, even when isolation seems safer. In short, joy returns when we start showing up, even when it's challenging—especially when it is difficult.

Often, the shift does not begin when you finally feel better, but when you stop looking inward and start moving outward. One of the most underrated, powerful medicines for depression is serving others. God has created a world in which even science confirms what Scripture has long shown: that intentional acts of serving others lift our spirits and lighten our mood. So, when you step into someone else's struggles, your own haze begins to lift, and your spirit finds footing again. You remember that in your weakness, God can work through you: the weight that felt immovable starts to loosen, one act of obedience at a time.

Scripture does not promise that we will feel strong all the time or that joy will always be evident. But it reminds us: *"They that sow in tears shall reap in joy"* (Psalm 126:5). Even your sorrow can become the soil where joy will eventually grow.

Healing takes time and trust. You do not have to fake a smile or pretend everything is all right. But you need to remember that God is still writing your story. He never leaves a story unfinished.

So do not measure your progress by the happiness you feel today. Measure it by the fact that you are still here, breathing, and willing to show up. You are still willing to believe (even if it's only a mustard seed of belief) that joy is possible again. Because it is.

You may not see the sunrise yet. But it is coming. And when it does, it will shine brighter because you chose to keep showing up, even at the hardest of times in life.

YOU ARE NOT THE DARKNESS

Maybe as you have been reading, something has stirred in your heart. Perhaps these words allowed you to understand the feelings you have carried but never knew how to express. Maybe you even teared up because the pain you have carried finally had a place to breathe. And somewhere you have found yourself thinking, *That's me. That's what I'm walking through right now.*

If that's true, I want to share with you something I wish

someone had spoken over me in my darkest hours: You are not the darkness you are passing through. You are not your heaviest thoughts. You are not the fog clouding your mind, the weight pressing on your chest, or the sadness that lingers without end. You are a beautiful creation of God, and you are loved, seen, and held, right here, right now.

Depression may be a chapter in your story, but it is not the whole book. It does not define your worth. It does not get to write the ending. That final word belongs to God, and here is what He says to you: *"Fear thou not; for I am with thee: be not dismayed; for I am thy God: I will strengthen thee; yea, I will help thee..."* (Isaiah 41:10).

You are not forgotten by God or by those who truly love you, and not by me either. Even if you feel empty, God can still use you right here and now, in the midst of your struggle. He is the God who brings beauty from ashes and sings over the broken. He is not finished with you.

So do not give up. Do not let the darkness convince you this is forever. You do not need to feel strong; you just need to keep going. Let each step be an act of defiance against despair. Let your perseverance become worship to God. Let your life, even in its lowest moments, declare to the enemy: "I'm still here. And God's not done with me yet." Because God is not finished, and He never will be.

13

GRIEF AND LOSS: THE DEEP HURT

You never expect the world to keep spinning after tragedy strikes. But somehow, it does. The neighbor still mows his lawn. The mail arrives on time. Someone laughs at something trivial in the store. And there you are, frozen, watching life carry on while yours has just shattered.

There is no simple way to talk about loss. Some losses are unbearable, the kind that mark us forever like the death of a child. No matter how many years pass, a piece of you remains frozen in that moment. You still hear their laughter. Their room might still be untouched; their birthday still marked on the calendar. Life keeps going, but a part of you never follows.

Sometimes grief comes in the absence of what you longed for: a pregnancy that never comes, a wedding ring taken off for the last time, or a dream you gave everything to but couldn't keep alive. Sometimes it crashes in suddenly. Sometimes it creeps in slowly until you are reminded that something precious is gone.

Grief is incredibly challenging because it often comes without warning and can feel suffocating. You try to pray, but the words stick in your throat. You try to sleep, but the anguish refuses to let you rest. You wonder how something so invisible can hurt so deeply. But it does because what you have lost mattered. Because love, when it has nowhere to go, can cause severe emotional pain.

Grief also rarely leaves us forever. It may subside or slip out of sight for a while, but it can come back, subtle yet persistent, marked by smaller moments of pain. You learn to smile again and to plan again, but the absence never disappears. It weaves itself into who you are.

Through every stage of grief, God sees it. Whether you have lost a child, a spouse, a parent, a friend, or just a piece of yourself, He has not turned away. And neither have I. You are not weak because you still cry. You are not faithless because you still ask why. You are human, and in that humanity, God draws near in the middle of your pain, offering you His tender loving kindness.

WHEN GOD'S TIMING FEELS WRONG

I still remember standing in the back of a chapel as an eighteen-year-old, sobbing uncontrollably. Not for my own grief, but for the mother of my dead friend, lying in the casket. Her screams pierced the air; the wail of a soul being ripped apart. The kind that makes you shiver as if hell itself had split open inside her chest. None of us could move. None of us could forget.

There is something profoundly unnatural about burying a child. Everything in you protests, *This is not how it's supposed to be.* It feels like they were taken too soon.

But that ache is not limited to a parent's grief. It is felt when a spouse dies in their thirties, when a man slips into eternity before holding his grandchild, or when a dream you've prayed and worked for shatters just as it was about to take shape. Different circumstances, yet all layered with the same haunting question: *Why now?*

And buried under that question is often a harder one: *God, if You're good... and if You're really in control... why would You let this happen?*

Thankfully, that question does not unsettle God. He is not offended by your pain. Your honesty does not shake Him. He does not flinch when your voice cracks in anger or despair. But He does remind us, gently and firmly, that His timing is not ours. *"For my thoughts are not your thoughts, neither are your ways my ways,"* He says in Isaiah 55, *"For as the heavens are higher than the earth, so are my ways higher than your ways, and my thoughts than your thoughts."*

At a graveside, this may hardly feel like comfort. When you wake up to an empty bed, or sit in silence where laughter used to be, God's *"higher ways"* may feel like a dagger than a healing balm. But it is the truth—sometimes the only force strong enough to steady us.

We can only see moments. God sees the whole story. We see what feels unfinished; He sees what is complete. His decisions may feel unbearable, but they are never arbitrary, careless, or cruel. They are the precise timing of an eternal God who has held the end in His hands from the very beginning.

Job put it this way: *"[Man's] days are determined, the number of his months are with thee, thou hast appointed his bounds that he cannot pass."* (Job 14:5). In other words, our days are not just counted; they are appointed.

So maybe the child you lost lived exactly the number of days God designed for him or her. Perhaps the death of your spouse, as painful as it was, lasted just long enough to teach you what ease never could. Maybe that door that closed so abruptly was God's way of shielding you from a future He never intended for you to carry. We may not understand it now. In fact, we probably will not. But one day, when time folds into eternity, I do not think we will argue with God. I think we will fall to our knees and cry out, "You were right."

Until then, it is okay to wrestle. It is okay to cry out, "Lord, this hurts." Even in that place of fear and sadness, He is with you, showing mercy in ways we sometimes cannot see yet.

WHEN GOD SPARES WHAT WE CAN'T SEE

There is a verse tucked in the book of Isaiah that never makes its way into sympathy cards or framed artwork. Yet for anyone who has lost someone too soon, it offers one of the most tender glimpses into the heart of God: *"The righteous perisheth, and no man layeth it to heart: and merciful men are taken away, none considering that the righteous is taken away from the evil to come"* (Isaiah 57:1).

What appears to us as tragedy may, in reality, be God's mercy. That is not something you announce at a funeral. You do not rush to tell this to a parent whose child has just passed on, or to a widow clutching her husband's shirt. This isn't meant to rush grief or silence tears. But in time, it can come as a tender word of comfort: *Maybe God was sparing them. Or maybe... sparing you.*

God sees what we cannot. In love, He may call loved ones Home early, like a Father shielding His child from a sorrow we will never know on this side of Heaven. From temptations that might have ensnared them. From pain that would have broken them. From choices that could have led them far from Him.

What if the little one you lost would have grown up in a world too harsh for their tender soul? What if the man you loved was spared from a suffering that would have stripped him of dignity and robbed you of peace? What if the relationship that fell apart was God's way of protecting you from something that looked good, but would have eventually destroyed you?

We imagine that more time would have healed. That just a few more years, a few more chances, could have made it better. But what if more time would have only deepened the wound? What if the mercy of God stepped in to shield us?

This does not erase the pain, quiet the longing in your heart, or stop the memories from ambushing you. But it gives grief somewhere to rest: in the goodness of a Father who never guesses, never gambles, and never gets it wrong. One day, you will see what He saw. And when you do, you may find that even your hardest goodbyes were wrapped in mercy.

Until then, the ache remains. The questions still arise. Wholeness still feels far away. Yet strangely, over time, grief itself begins to grow into a deepening of your faith.

WHEN GRIEF GROWS FAITH

When grief first appears, it feels like it has pulled the rug out from under us, leaving us clutching at air, desperate for something solid. It tears open what we thought was secure, exposing the fragile places we did not even know existed. Suddenly, we are not only mourning what we lost; we are questioning everything we thought we knew.

And yet, in that hollow space, I have seen something holy take root. I have watched parents bury a child and still cling to God, not because they understood Him, but because they had nowhere else to run. They never "got over it," yet in the wreckage, they learned to walk with Him in a new way.

I have seen it in a woman sitting beside her husband as cancer slowly steals him away, in a man who walked away from a crash that takes his best friend, and in a grandmother whose failing body strips her of independence. Each story reaches a breaking point. In that raw cry for God, something sacred often begins. Grief does not usually hand us answers. But it can hand us God, who sits with us in the ashes. He offers no shortcuts to healing, but He offers Himself.

Faith is not forged in comfort. It is born in the ruins. In the stillness after the storm. In the prayer too broken for words. In the moment, you do not know how to take another breath.

Before loss, we leaned on routines, relationships, and the illusion of control. Grief strips those supports away until all that remains is the Rock beneath it all. And when we land on Him, we discover He is enough.

It is then that this ancient promise takes on flesh and bone: *"The LORD is nigh unto them that are of a broken heart; and saveth such as be of a contrite spirit"* (Psalm 34:18).

The people I have met with the deepest, most unshakable faith did not find it sitting in church pews. They found it in the wilderness of significant loss, walking with God in the fires of adversity. And when they speak, you can feel the weight in their words, the tenderness in their worship, and the gravity in their prayers.

That kind of faith is not cheap. It may wobble. It may wrestle. Yet it endures because it is built on clinging to God when everything else is gone. If you are still shaking, questioning *why*, and struggling to breathe through the wreckage, please know that your grief is not a detour from God. It may be the very soil where your roots sink deeper into Him. And as strange as it sounds, what begins to grow in you may one day give life to others, too.

WHEN GRIEF INSPIRES OTHERS TO SERVE

Sometimes the most beautiful acts of love are born out of the deepest pain. Grief has a peculiar way of opening eyes that used to look away and softening hearts once guarded. Something breaks, and self-compassion, along with compassion for others, begins to flourish. I have seen churches respond this way, much like individuals do—with meals and flowers, and people who show up, offering presence without trying to rush the pain away. The tears of one person can awaken an entire community to action.

That is more than comfort; it is obedience and a calling. Galatians 6:2 calls us to *"Bear ye one another's burdens, and so fulfil the law of Christ."*

Even after the calls stop coming, the meals stop arriving, and the world slips back into routine, I have met people who let their sorrow bloom into something lasting. A support group for mothers who have lost babies. A mentorship program for boys without fathers. A ministry of presence for the lonely.

Grief did not destroy them. It equipped them. It did not make them weaker; it made them willing to walk through trials and tribulations alongside others because they know the feeling well.

If you are grieving, you may not feel strong enough to help anyone right now. That's okay. You're not supposed to fix anything. Just breathe. But after you have processed and healed enough to look outward, and you feel that quiet nudge to let pain become purpose, follow it. You do not need to be fully healed to be helpful. You only need to be willing.

If you are walking beside someone in grief, unsure of what to say, do not worry. You do not have to speak profound words. Just show up. Sit with them. Stay. Serve quietly. Love faithfully. Your presence matters. Sometimes it is the very lifeline God uses to keep them going.

Grief may have broken something in you, but it can also awaken something in someone else. And when that happens, when your experience of sorrow inspires how you live, it becomes a vital and powerful testimony.

WHEN SUFFERING BECOMES A TESTIMONY

There is a kind of faith that does not need a microphone. It is the mother who shows up to church just days after burying her child. Her trembling hands are lifted in worship, tears streaming down her face, as she tells God, "You are still good." That faith preaches more than any sermon ever could, for the way she holds grief speaks volumes. It lives in the quiet resolve to keep showing up. To keep praising. To keep trusting, even when everything inside wants to collapse in despair.

It doesn't mean putting on a mask of strength. It doesn't mean pretending you are fine. It means saying through tears, "God, I still believe."

Jesus never avoided suffering. He wept. He bled. He felt forsaken. Yet through His pain came redemption. The cross was the world's darkest day, but it was also the dawn of hope. If God could bring resurrection from that, then He can bring something beautiful from ours, too.

You may not feel like a testimony right now. You may feel numb, disoriented, and worn thin. Yet simply by holding on and not giving up on God, you bear witness to something eternal.

When others see you pray for them even while your own prayers seem unanswered... when they notice you serve through tears or speak words of kindness in the midst of grief... when they watch you keep walking with Jesus, even when walking away would be easier... they begin to wonder whether He really is enough.

Your suffering can speak to others, showing them a faith that continues to lean on and trust God. It is through enduring trust that the Gospel shines through with its greatest power.

THE GOSPEL IN EVERY LOSS

Grief has a way of stripping life down to its rawest questions. Suddenly, the thoughts you once tucked away rise to the surface. *Why did this happen? Where is God? What happens now?* When someone you love is taken too soon, eternity ceases to be a distant thought. It becomes urgent and personal, which is precisely the place where the Gospel of Jesus Christ speaks loudest.

This world is broken. We feel it each time we stand beside a hospital bed or kneel at a fresh grave. This is not how it was meant to be. Death, sorrow, and separation were never part of God's original design. But when sin entered the world, it fractured what was once whole, and we have been grieving ever since. This is why the Gospel is not only good news for sinners; it is good news for the sorrowful as well.

Jesus did not remain distant from our pain. He wept at Lazarus's tomb. He touched the untouchable. He bore our sickness and shame, and carried all of it to the cross. Scripture puts it plainly: *"Surely he hath borne our griefs, and carried our sorrows"* (Isaiah 53:4).

Jesus did not die only for what we have done; He died for every injustice, every wound, and every loss we have experienced. And when He rose again, He broke the very grip of death itself.

That means Jesus gets the last word. *"I am the resurrection, and the life: he that believeth in me, though he were dead, yet shall he live"* (John 11:25).

Because of the resurrection, our tears are not wasted. Our goodbyes are not forever. One day, graves will be emptied. One day, the child you lost will be in your arms again. One day, there will be no more hospitals or funerals. Only joy found through Jesus. Yet the Gospel is not just about someday; it is also about *today*. It means you are not alone, even now. The same Saviour who conquered death walks beside you in this wilderness. His Spirit strengthens you. His comfort surrounds you. His promises hold, even while you wait.

If your grief has pushed you to the edge of faith, then let me assure you that you are closer to healing than you realize. Jesus is right there with you, right now. He loves you so deeply that He would never allow you to bear this pain all alone.

14

HEALING
FROM SEXUAL ABUSE

Whether or not you have been affected by sexual abuse, I want to gently invite you to listen in and try to understand. To weep with those who have wept. And to become a safe place for someone who has. Because someone you know may still be silently carrying this pain. And maybe God is preparing you to be the one who does not look away.

Sexual abuse is a terrible psychological and emotional wound. It does not just scar the body. It fractures trust. It distorts identity. It steals the sense of ever being "normal" again.

It is a wound that follows you home, crawls under your blanket, and seeps into your pillow at night. It whispers words no one should ever hear: *Don't tell anyone. No one will believe you. This is your fault.*

If you have lived through abuse, you know that confusion well. It does not only come from the abuser; it burrows into your soul. It wraps itself around your voice until you do not know how to speak at all.

I know, because I lived it. As a young boy, I was sexually abused. I did not understand it at the time, and I certainly did not have words for it. All I knew was that something inside me was different. I did not know how to explain it, so I buried it deep, covering it with layers of confusion. As a child, the distortion within cut me so deep that even the truth began to sound like a lie, so I hid from my experience. But hiding it has a way of turning into anger, frustration, shame, and identity struggles that resurface years later.

If you have walked that road or anything like it, please know: you are not alone. I am not here to offer neat explanations for why it happened to you or someone you love. I do not have those answers. I am here to sit with you in the aftermath. To remind you that even in the questions, even in the terrible pain you have carried, God has not abandoned you.

Even now, as an adult, there are parts of my own story I do not fully understand. Writing these words hasn't been easy. I still feel inadequate to speak on something so heavy, because I, too, continue to bring unanswered questions to God. But I have walked through the shame. I have wrestled with identity struggles. I have carried raw anger. I have endured many nights wrestling with doubt and torment. And somehow, by grace, He has walked with me every step of the way.

Many survivors never speak a word. Some tried, but no one believed them. Others still wonder if they will ever feel clean again. If that is your experience, then you need to know that you are not what was done to you; you are not just a victim; and you are more than a survivor. You are an overcomer, and your story is still being written, with the power to impact others.

NOT YOUR SHAME

If you have been sexually abused, one of the heaviest burdens you may carry is shame, which has a way of seeping into places the abuser never even touched. It poisons your self-worth, distorts the way you see yourself, and convinces you that you were the one who did something wrong, even though you were not. That shame, which has clung to you all these years, is not yours to carry.

Shame is one of Satan's most powerful weapons. He uses it to muzzle victims into silence, filling them with the fear of being exposed because they have been sinned against in such an intimate way. In that fear, many of us, myself included, learned to survive by hiding. Not just the story, but ourselves.

That was how my abuse worked. My abuser was someone trusted by my family, welcomed into our home again and again. I was a child with neither the cynicism nor the context to understand what was happening. I had no idea it was wrong, because it was cloaked in familiarity and whispered secrecy, which made it feel as though I was protecting us by keeping it quiet.

Even years later, I still felt unsettled because I had been sinned against in the most personal of ways. I felt conflicted about what had been touched and what parts of me were seen. Because it was my body, parts already wrapped in modesty and privacy, the disorientation only deepened.

But here is what I have learned in the many decades since then:

The shame of what was done to you is not yours. It belongs to the one who did it. And even deeper still, Jesus understands. He was once publicly humiliated: stripped, spit on, and hung on a cross, completely naked, while others mocked and stared.

The Bible says Jesus *"endured the cross, despising the shame"* (Hebrews 12:2). The cross was more than physical torture. It was meant to degrade Him and cover Him in shame. And He bore that shame so you would never have to.

If you are a survivor of sexual abuse, I want you to know that you share in a unique part of Christ's suffering. He knows what it feels like to be violated, humiliated, and exposed. He is not ashamed to stand beside you.

The enemy wants to use shame to destroy you. But the Spirit of God speaks the truth: you are not dirty, ruined, or beyond healing. You are beloved, you are seen, and in Christ, you are whole.

WHY DOES GOD ALLOW IT?

Surviving abuse is difficult enough. But the confusion, the silence of Heaven, and the pain of not understanding why a good God would allow something so evil can haunt you for years afterward.

I have wrestled with this more times than I can count within the quiet corners of my soul. There is a sacred discomfort that settles in when you realize God could have stopped something and did not. You are left staring at your faith, wondering what to do with beliefs that suddenly feel disjointed.

I never believed God was the one who hurt me. But I did wonder why He let it happen. As I grew older, the questions multiplied: Why didn't He intervene? Why did He allow it to shape me?

Those questions stayed with me for years, as wounds bleeding into my faith, my relationships, and my calling. In my early twenties, I walked away from God for a while. Yet even then, He never let me go. He patiently pursued me and wouldn't let me bury the deeper questions.

I tried to push forward, to tell myself I had moved on. But unresolved pain always finds its way to the surface. It seeps into your trust, erodes your worth, and seeps into the way you love. You can numb it; or face it. Eventually, I couldn't keep numbing it. The shift within me began slowly, as God started showing me that I was asking the wrong question.

Around the age of twenty-five, it became unmistakably clear. My heart kept crying, "Why, God?" But instead of answering, He turned me toward a better question: "Lord, what do You want me to do?"

That question changed everything. God did not erase the past or untangle every mystery. But when I stopped demanding explanations and started asking what He wanted to do with my pain, the healing began. Over the course of many years, He opened my wounded heart to forgiveness, gave me a deeper understanding of who He is, and filled my life with purpose I never expected. He brought hurting people across my path, and somehow, my scars became part of their healing too.

I still do not know why He allowed it. But I have stopped mistaking His silence with absence. And I have stopped waiting for a perfect answer when He is already offering His presence, His Word, and a calling that makes my broken story matter. Healing has taken time. Forgiveness has taken time. But the moment I stopped clinging to answers, I began to find direction. Sometimes the breakthrough does not come through clarity but through surrender.

THE BODY REMEMBERS

The human body is a sacred mystery, etched with both God's glory and our frailty. It is wonderfully complex, tender, and intricate. It holds memory in ways even modern science is only beginning to understand. Long after your mind forgets, or tries to, your body still remembers.

That is one of the most complex issues about healing from sexual abuse. You can forgive. You can surrender the pain to God. You can walk in freedom. But then, out of nowhere, your body reacts. A smell. A familiar room. A stranger's face that looks a little too much like the one you once saw. And suddenly, you are pulled back by instinct. That does not mean you are broken. It means you are human.

For some survivors, even a casual touch or an innocent interaction can unleash a tidal wave of emotion. Your chest tightens. Your senses flare. Your thoughts spiral. You do not want it, but there it is: your body keeping score of what it survived.

I was unaware of this for many years. I thought maybe I had not healed, perhaps that I was still messed up. But the truth is that healing is not always a linear process. Trauma is layered and lives in your skin, in your muscles, and in your nervous system. Your body may still remember what your soul is learning to release, and that's okay.

Sometimes those aftershocks are not always fear; they are unwanted desires. That's the part we rarely talk about but need to, because when abuse awakens sexuality before your soul is ready, it distorts everything. It lights a fire too soon. And for some of us, that fire didn't go out; it grew.

In the years after my abuse, I sometimes felt drawn toward what had once wounded me. I had thoughts I did not understand and feelings that confused and alarmed me. There were moments I felt pulled toward male bodies, and I did not know what to make of it. But those were not temptations so much as echoes of responses awakened before their time—not born of choice, but of distortions. I have learned since that those confusing feelings did not define me. They were not my identity; they were symptoms of something stolen too soon, tangled up in trauma.

Confusion is a cruel weight survivors often carry, wired for intimacy but distorted by pain. For a long time, I thought I might be too damaged to heal, that maybe my desires proved I was broken. But over the years, I have learned that God is not afraid of our twisted places, and He does not flinch at our scars. Healing is possible; it just takes time. Sometimes it comes through the steady presence of a godly counselor, a trauma-informed pastor, or a Spirit-filled community that knows how to listen and walk with you slowly.

If you are going through something similar, know that you are not crazy, you're not a pervert, you're not faithless, and you're not alone in this. Jesus knows what it is like to carry trauma in a body. He bore our griefs, carried our sorrows, and was brutally beaten at the hands of soldiers before He walked up to the cross. Even in His resurrected glory, He kept the scars because they have been redeemed. If you belong to Him, your body is not defined by what it remembers. You are defined by the One who redeemed you—spirit, soul, and body;

the One who heals layer by layer; the One who speaks, "You are My beloved. And I am making all things new."

WHEN THE ACHE LINGERS

Sometimes you don't realize how heavy the load is until God places someone in your path who carries a similar wound. That happened years after my abuse, long after I was no longer a child. The turning point did not come through therapy, or a book, or even a sermon. It came in my early thirties while I was sitting with orphans in Mexico who had suffered abuses no child should ever endure. As the teenagers shared their stories and I listened, something inside me cracked open. Their brokenness began to soften mine. Their voices gave language to what I had buried. Their tears gave me permission to feel my own.

It was the first time I sensed that God might not just be asking me to survive the past but to see it redeemed. For a long time, I thought healing meant the pain would disappear; that one day I would wake up free from old thoughts, finally whole, and unharmed, untouched by what once broke me. But real healing is not like that. It is not a finish line; it is a slow, holy *becoming*.

Even now, there are days when the battle rages. Thoughts slip in uninvited. My body reacts in ways I wish it would not. Memories surface at the worst times. I've prayed against them, surrendered them, fought them, and sometimes they still linger.

For a long time, I assumed that meant I had not truly healed. But I have learned that healing and struggle are not opposites; they often live side by side. My identity is not in the struggle, but in the grace that meets me there. And that is the grace I want to extend to others.

The truth is, your story is not over because it is messy. You are not disqualified because you still wrestle. Weakness does not cancel your witness; it deepens it. Ministry often begins in the broken places that God is still redeeming. So, if you feel disqualified because of past experiences, please know that God is not finished with you. He is still writing your story. And He is not afraid of the chapters you'd rather skip.

WHEN THE WOUND IS DISMISSED

Not every wound comes from what was done to you. Sometimes, the deeper cut comes later, when you finally find the courage to speak, and the response makes you wish you never had.

Perhaps you confided in someone you trusted, such as a friend, mentor, or pastor. You were not asking for pity or revenge. You just wanted to be seen and heard and to have someone say they believe you. But instead, they hesitated. They asked prying questions. They told you not to dwell on the past. Or worse, they tossed out a quick "Just forgive and forget," as if that's all Jesus would expect.

That kind of dismissal stings and rattles your sense of reality. It makes you second-guess your own story. *Was I wrong to speak up? Was it really abuse? Am I overreacting?*

I have known people who have been told to "move on," "cheer up," or "quote more Scripture." Some were made to feel like the problem was them, as if they were too sensitive, too bitter, or too complicated. And when those messages come from inside the church, the wound cuts deeper and can distort your view of God. Because if His people do not take your pain seriously, maybe He does not either. That is the lie that seeps into your soul.

But hear me when I say that God does not and will not ever dismiss you. He is not rolling His eyes at your story. He is not scolding you for still hurting. He is not embarrassed by how long it is taking you to heal.

Jesus is nothing like the ones who silenced you. He never shames the suffering. He draws near to them. *"A bruised reed shall he not break,"* the Bible says, *"and the smoking flax shall he not quench"* (Isaiah 42:3). He does not rush you to get better. He sits with you while it still hurts. He does not demand that you tidy up your grief before He will enter it.

If Scripture was twisted to shame you, that was not God's voice. If forgiveness was used to silence you, that was not the Spirit's leading. If someone made you feel like your pain was a burden to the church, then that was never the heart of Christ. God's love does not come with a stopwatch. His healing does not come with a script. And His nearness does not depend on whether others understood your pain. You do not have to hide your story to belong to Him. If the church hurt you instead of helping you, I am deeply sorry. You deserved better, and I believe Jesus Himself would say the same.

But please, do not give up on the body of Christ because of the failures of a few. Not every Christian will mishandle your pain. Not every church will turn away. There are still men and women who are Spirit-led and tenderhearted who know how to sit with sorrow without rushing it, who will weep with you, walk with you, and remind you of your worth without a trace of shame.

God has not abandoned the church. He still delights in using His people to bring comfort and hope. And even now, He may be preparing someone to walk with you in ways that others could not.

So do not let a painful response convince you that silence is safer. Your story is part of your healing, and God can use it, not only to restore you but to bring healing to others.

The failures of a few do not erase the fellowship and love He still desires to give you through His people. There is a way forward, and it begins by believing that your story is worth telling, your voice is worth hearing, and your healing is worth pursuing. Because *you* are worth it to the One who never dismissed you. And now, as impossible as it may seem, we must discuss the next step: forgiveness.

FINDING FORGIVENESS

There is a part of healing almost no one feels ready for—a place that can feel too steep, too unfair, and too soon: Forgiveness. Even the word can sting, especially when the wound is fresh and when no one has said, "I'm sorry."

When I first began to grasp how another had wronged me, I was bewildered. As the memories settled in and reality became clear, I found myself standing face-to-face with the call to forgive. I did not know where to begin. *How do I even do that? What about justice? What about answers?* I wanted to scream, asking God to explain. And in the midst of all that noise, I was gently reminded of grace, even for those who had shattered something inside me.

In that moment, I do not believe God was rushing me. He was patient, present, and kind. Forgiveness is not something you fake or force. It is something God invites you into, but He does not shame you into it. What helped me was Jesus Himself, slowly and gently meeting me in my pain, showing me what forgiveness really is and what it is not.

Forgiveness is not saying what they did was alright. It is not pretending it did not matter. It is not trusting them again, reconciling with them, nor even confronting them face-to-face. It is simply releasing a burden that your soul was never meant to carry. I used to think forgiveness was about the person being forgiven. But now I know, it is about me stepping out of the prison of bitterness and letting God hold what I was never designed to bear.

There came a point in my healing where I realized I was still tethered by anger to the persons who hurt me. They still had their grip on me, my mind telling me that they "still owed me." But the longer I held on, the more it consumed me, shaped me, and defined me. Then Jesus tenderly spoke something to my heart that changed everything: *"I died for that pain too."*

He was not excusing the abuse or minimizing the wound. He was offering to take on what I could not. Eventually, the day came when I chose something different for myself with trembling honesty: "God, I forgive them." It did not feel like closure or some grand, heroic act. It felt raw and unfinished, but it was real. In that moment, I felt the first tug of the chain begin to loosen. Forgiveness did not erase the trauma, nor did it undo the years of confusion, anger, and ache. But it made space for God to start building something new where only rubble had been before.

And let me be clear: forgiveness is not a one-time event. It is a process, and not an easy one. There are days I have had to forgive again (and maybe a few times after that) because the pain would resurface in a new way. When that happens, I know I have to bring it back to Jesus because I need Him to remind me: *"I understand. I see it all. Let Me carry this."*

If you are not there yet, that's okay. Jesus is not angry with your hesitation. He is not rushing your timeline. He knows what it costs you. When you are ready, He will walk with you into a forgiveness that is freeing for you.

So don't picture forgiveness as letting someone off the hook. Picture it as letting yourself off the hook of being the judge, jury, and executioner. Picture it as standing in the presence of a Saviour, who was abused, mocked, stripped, and died, and still said, *"Father, forgive them."* Jesus did this because it was the only way to break the curse of bitterness, self-destruction, and ultimately, sin.

Right now, Jesus is offering you and me forgiveness that says: You are not what they did to you. You are not owned by anger. You are not trapped in bitterness. You are free to breathe again and live again, and to become who you were always meant to be: whole, holy, and deeply held by the God who knows what it is like to forgive the unforgivable.

THE WOUND WAS REAL...
BUT SO IS THE VICTORY

There was a time I believed I would always be defined by what happened to me. That no matter how much I prayed, served, or healed, there would always be this invisible label stamped across my life: *Tainted. Unclean.* I held this idea, tucked behind smiles and even my faith in Jesus.

However, something changed over time as I began to see myself through God's Word, rather than through the lens of my pain. I realized: I am not what they did to me. I am not the desires I never asked for. I am not the silence of others or the shame I once bore. Instead, I am redeemed, restored, and beloved. And I am *not* a victim.

The Bible defines who I am: *"Therefore if any man be in Christ, he is a new creature: old things are passed away; behold, all things are become new"* (2 Corinthians 5:17).

That is my reality. And it can be yours too.

Abuse may have marked your life, but it does not get the final say. You may hold onto memories that still sting, or wounds that surface from time to time. But those experiences do not define you. They are part of your story, yes, but they are not who you are. The devil revels in taunting that you are forever stained, forever disqualified, forever dirty. But Jesus speaks louder and with the authority that you are redeemed, brave, and beloved.

You did not ask for this battle. But by God's grace, you are still here and still standing. God has a way of using the places we have been wounded to bring life to others. He takes the ashes we never wanted and shapes beauty we never thought possible. That does not mean the past disappears, but that the past no longer owns your future.

You are not weak for having struggled. You are strong for still believing, hoping, and still pressing forward, even when your voice shakes or your hands tremble. You are living proof that evil does not get the last word. You are not alone. You are not too far gone. And you are not what happened to you.

You are not a victim; you are a survivor capable of thriving. This is not where hope runs out. This is where healing takes root, where purpose begins to bloom. So, keep walking, even if it is with a limp, even if it is one small step at a time. You are not just surviving anymore; you are overcoming, and the world needs to hear your voice.

15

BRUISED BY WORDS

You can try to outrun a rumor, but it still finds you in the dark. I know, because I have lived it. There was a time in my life when my very name felt hijacked, tied to someone villainous, shameful, and unrecognizable. Conversations stopped when I entered the room. People I once laughed with started looking through me. And behind the silence, one question pulsed underneath the surface: *Had they heard?*

I would scroll through old texts, staring at names that had gone quiet. I could only speculate as to why they vanished, wondering what they now believed. The pain did not come from a blow to the body. It came from rumors that never stopped echoing. Such suffering is strange, isn't it? It's as if your story gets rewritten in places where your voice was never invited. You weren't confronted or given a chance to speak. You were quietly erased because someone chose to narrate your life in their words, handing their version to strangers and former friends.

Gossip. Slander. Misrepresentation. Whether it came dressed

as twisted truths or outright lies, the damage is the same: a bruised soul and a heart full of burning questions. *Why would they say that? Why didn't someone defend me? Why is God letting this happen?*

I have asked everyone those questions. You may be asking them right now. If so, let's sit in this together like two old friends. I want to share with you that I've learned slander is both an attack *and* a test. And if we let God, He can shape something sacred out of what others meant to break.

THE MIRROR NO ONE WANTS TO FACE

Before I can talk any further about the wounds others have caused, I need to face something in myself that still grieves me. It is easy to point to the pain others have inflicted, but if we are honest, sometimes we have caused some of that pain too. I know I have. I haven't just been a victim of gossip; I have also passed it on. Not always with malice, and not intentionally--but I have certainly been careless and thoughtless with my words a little too often. I have repeated stories I did not fully understand. I have passed along someone else's story as if it were my own to tell. I have chimed in when silence would have been wiser. And I justified it with those dangerous little phrases like, "I'm just concerned," or "We need to pray for..." However, the truth is I was not praying; I was spreading. It was not helpful. It was ungodly. It was wrong.

I did not grasp the violence of gossip until I found myself on the other side of it. Suddenly, I knew what it felt like to become a headline in conversations I was never invited to join. To watch assumptions multiply faster than questions. To sense that people were content speaking *about* me instead of *to* me.

It Is Enough!

That is when it hit me: gossip is never harmless. It wounds through tone, suggestion, or the slightest twist of the truth. It can wreck friendships, poison churches, and plant seeds of suspicion that grow into full-grown division. All while someone casually shrugs, "I was just passing it along." But behind every comment is a real soul made in God's image, and our words can leave scars that linger long after we forget them.

That realization humbled me; and set me free. Through my pain, God began reshaping my heart. He did not just confront me with what others had done to me; He showed me what I had done to others. Slowly, He taught me to ask better questions before opening my mouth. *Is this my story to tell? Would I say this if the person were here? Am I actually helping, or just spreading?*

More often than not, I discovered that what I needed was not a bigger platform to speak, but a quieter place to pray. Now, when someone's name comes up, especially when it is someone who has fallen or is struggling, I try to pause and let God be the Judge instead of inserting myself. Their sin is not mine to expose. Their failures are not mine to dissect. Their journey belongs to God.

Curiously enough, the more I have learned to hold my tongue, the more I have learned to hear God's voice more clearly. I once came across a phrase that struck me deeply: "Gossip is confessing other people's sins." When we are busy spotlighting someone else's mess, we are usually trying to distract from our own faults or failures. But the Gospel invites us to come out of hiding—not by dragging others into the light, but by stepping into the light ourselves.

And when we do, we stop obsessing over what others are doing and start caring more about who we are becoming. God takes even the mess we have made with our words and, if we let Him, turns it into wisdom. He retrains the tongue that once spread poison to speak blessings instead. Sometimes, He even redeems the pain we have caused or endured, making our hearts tender enough to help others heal.

So, if gossip has stained your lips, take courage; you are not beyond grace. Healing begins in humility. Freedom flows through repentance. And joy comes when our words turn from poison into prayer. When the Holy Spirit softens your speech, He also softens your heart, and peace takes root in the places where anger once lived.

CHARACTER MATTERS MORE THAN REPUTATION

There is something uniquely terrifying about watching your reputation crumble, especially when you know you cannot stop it. You spend years trying to walk in integrity, doing your best to stay humble, serve, love, and follow Christ faithfully. And then all it takes is one accusation, one skewed version of your story, one person eager to believe the worst. Suddenly, your name is no longer your own. It has been redefined by someone else's words.

I have felt that grief. I have wept over remarks said about me, statements that cut to the bone. I have wrestled with the urge to fix it by telling my side and defending myself, and, if I am honest, to retaliate. To make them feel what I was feeling.

But while wrestling with those feelings, I began to see something I had missed before: reputation and character are not the same thing. Reputation is fragile. It lives in the opinions of others, and it can topple with a single sentence. Character is different. Character is who you are before God when no one else is looking. It does not crumble under gossip. It does not need applause to stand. It stands because Christ is its foundation. Often, the only way we truly discover the difference is by losing one and clinging to the other.

That's why slander, painful as it is, can become one of God's most refining tools. It strips away the illusion that we can control what others think. It forces us to ask where our worth truly lies. And it calls us to shift our focus from guarding an image to cultivating a soul.

Sometimes slander is outright lies. But sometimes it is more complicated. Sometimes it is laced with truth—exaggerated, distorted, yet still rooted in something real. That's the kind that hurts the most. Because it brushes against failures you already regret. It drags into the light mistakes you had hoped were long buried.

I have lived through those, too. There are errors I wish I could undo, words I wish I could take back. Seasons of life when I did not walk blamelessly, and others learned about it. Some misunderstood. Some exploited. Some twisted the truth into something far worse.

Through all of this, I had to learn a painful lesson: my failures did not justify the slander, and the slander did not cancel God's work in me. God is less concerned with salvaging our reputation than with sanctifying our hearts. He is not in the business of polishing our image; He is forming Christ in us. And often, that formation runs deepest in the very moments we are misrepresented, misunderstood, and knocked down.

I used to fight so hard to be understood. I thought if people just knew the whole story, they would see me differently. But in that struggle, God began breathing into my spirit: *Let Me be your defender. You focus on being faithful.*

That shift changed everything. It did not erase the pain, but it gave the pain a purpose. I stopped praying for vindication and started praying for formation. I stopped begging for people to see me rightly and began asking God to shape me rightly. Little by little, He began rebuilding my character; not my reputation.

So, if your name has been dragged through the dirt—if you are trapped in lies, assumptions, or twisted half-truths—know this: you are not your reputation. You are not what they say. You are who you are before the Lord. He sees the whole story. Your past does not rattle him, and He is not finished with your future.

Let slander drive you to your knees rather than into the court of public approval. Let it peel away the hunger to be seen and anchor your identity firmly in Christ. You do not have to get them back. You do not have to persuade everyone. You only have to walk upright before the Lord, one day at a time. And in the end, He will finish the work He began in you because your heart stayed yielded to Him. In that hidden place, where reputation falls away, you may find what you did not even know you needed: peace.

WHEN THEIR WORDS REVEAL THEIR WOUNDS

The pain of slander cuts deep. It is personal. Someone twists your story, assumes your motives, or labels you without ever asking a question. Suddenly, you are left bleeding from a wound you did not cause. Over time, I have learned that slander reveals more about the person speaking than about the person being spoken about. The tongue is a mirror, reflecting what's hidden in the heart. Jesus said it plainly: *"for out of the abundance of the heart the mouth speaketh"* (Matthew 12:34).

When someone spreads gossip, it usually reveals something unsettled within them: hurt, bitterness, insecurity, envy, pride, or a need to feel superior or exert control. That does not excuse the damage, but it shifts how we see it. When I began to recognize slander not only as an attack but also as a symptom of someone else's unrest, I received two unexpected gifts: clarity and compassion.

Clarity kept me from internalizing every accusation and helped me realize that this is not all about me; something is broken in them, too. Compassion was harder because it required surrender. But that is where healing begins, because I realized I had a choice. I could let the wound harden me—making me sharp, guarded, and suspicious—or I could let the wound soften me. Compassion lets us say, "I won't let your words poison my spirit, but I will pray for you anyway." It's not easy, but it is righteous.

King David exemplified this heart when he wrote: *"Let the righteous smite me; it shall be a kindness: and let him reprove me; it shall be an excellent oil, which shall not break my head: for yet my prayer also shall be in their calamities"* (Psalm 141:5). David chose prayer over revenge, surrendering the right to strike back, and through that surrender, his heart stayed tender before God.

David's example ultimately points us to the greater One: Jesus Himself. He put it plainly: *"Love your enemies, bless them that curse you, do good to them that hate you, and pray for them which despitefully use you"* (Matthew 5:44). As nails pierced His hands and slander filled the air, He lived those very words, showing us how to respond when wrongly treated: *"Father, forgive them; for they know not what they do"* (Luke 23:34). That kind of prayer is supernatural. It does not excuse wrong, but it frees the wounded heart from bitterness.

Sometimes the most powerful response to slander is intercession. In that difficult obedience, peace begins to blossom. That does not mean we excuse slander. It means we refuse to be hardened by it. We let it drive us, not to anger, but to our knees. I am not responsible for healing the one who slandered me. But I am responsible for guarding my own heart. And that is where God meets us: in the quiet place where forgiveness is chosen.

In the end, I would rather carry a soft heart and a bruised name than protect a polished reputation with a bitter soul. Let their words reveal their hearts, and let your response reveal Christ in yours.

WHEN YOU WANT TO REACT BUT GOD INVITES YOU TO RESPOND

When someone slanders you, everything in you wants to fight back. You hear your name being dragged through the mud, and your first instinct is to set the record straight. We want our reputation back, and we want it now. We want the slanderer silenced and the pain undone. I have been there. I have typed the unsent emails. Rehearsed the conversations in my head. Picked up the phone to yell, only to hang up before I made a fool of myself.

But God rarely invites us to fight. Instead, He calls us to something harder. Something holier. Restraint—a silence born of surrender. Reacting is fast and fueled by emotional pain. And while it might feel justified in the moment, it often spreads the damage further. Responding, however, is slower. Prayerful. Filtered through grace. It does not deny the wounds; it refuses to let pain speak for us.

The tension between reacting and responding is not new. It has followed God's people for generations, pressing on the same nerve again and again. Few lives reveal it more clearly than David's. Slander was a constant companion throughout his life. Long before he wore a crown, he was hunted by King Saul, mocked, misrepresented, and branded a traitor. Years later, as king, the very people David was called to shepherd turned against him with bitter false accusations.

One particular moment from David's early years captures this struggle with piercing clarity. King Saul had pursued him relentlessly, spreading lies to justify his hatred. Then, in a twist David could never have planned, Saul, alone and vulnerable, entered the cave where David was hiding. David's men leaned in, whispering, "This is your chance." By every human measure, the moment seemed justified. The injustice demanded revenge.

But David chose restraint: *"The Lord forbid that I should stretch forth mine hand against the Lord's anointed,"* he said (1 Samuel 26:11). He refused to let Saul's sins dictate his integrity. David would not trade his calling for revenge, not even when it would have been easy.

This was not hesitation. It was faithfulness rooted in trust. David knew what God had promised for his life did not need to be seized by force. Instead of reacting, he chose to respond by waiting, placing the outcome in God's hands rather than acting on impulse. In the cave's darkness, restraint became an act of faith.

And then there is Jesus.

When Jesus faced slander and false accusations, He did not lash out. Scripture says, *"And when he was accused of the chief priests and elders, he answered nothing... And he answered him to never a word; insomuch that the governor marvelled greatly"* (Matthew 27:12-14). His silence was not resignation; it was trust—resting in the Father to enact justice, even when human judgment failed.

That gives us hope when we are misrepresented as well. Jesus' intention was not to be understood; it was to be faithful. That's the invitation God offers us in the face of slander: not a silence that leaves us feeling powerless, but a stillness that places our power in the hands of the One who sees it all.

I am not suggesting we must always remain silent. Sometimes, the truth must be told. Boundaries must be set. Silence can even become a kind of lie when justice is at stake. But too often, we rush to defend ourselves before asking the Lord what He desires. In our haste, we miss the deeper work God is accomplishing in us.

When we choose that stillness as an act of worship, God begins transforming the turmoil in our hearts into trust. Now, when the fire rises in my chest… when the sting of betrayal tempts my hand to grab the phone, I pause. I get alone with God. I ask, "Lord, is this mine to answer, or Yours to handle?" And when He nudges, *Be still*, I try to listen. Sometimes, the greatest strength is not in speaking loudly but in trusting deeply.

WHEN SLANDER TRIES
TO DISTRACT YOU FROM YOUR PURPOSE

Slander does not just injure, it interrupts. It pulls your attention away from your life's calling and tempts you to pause your journey. If you have ever been misrepresented, you know how consuming it can be. You lie awake, replaying conversations in your head. You scroll through old contact lists, searching for someone who still believes in you. You begin to withdraw because defending yourself feels endless and exhausting.

Slowly, often without realizing it, your purpose begins to blur. The devil does not need to destroy your life mission, he only needs to distract you from it. David understood this danger firsthand. Opposition tested not only his character; it tested whether he would retaliate or allow it to pull him off course.

Long years into his reign as king, David faced the same test again while fleeing Jerusalem during his son Absalom's rebellion. A man named Shimei followed him, shouting curses, hurling stones, and publicly slandering him. David's men were ready to strike. But David stopped them: *"...let him alone, and let him curse; for the LORD hath bidden him. It may be that the LORD will look on mine affliction, and that the LORD will requite me good for his cursing this day"* (2 Samuel 16:11-12).

That was not weakness; it was profound trust. David understood what most of us struggle to accept: not every attack deserves our attention. God already sees it. Rather than defending his reputation, David guarded his character, trusting God to bring good where others meant harm.

Jesus held that same kind of unwavering focus. Through every accusation, insult, and misrepresentation, He kept His eyes on the cross. He did not stop healing. He did not stop loving. He did not pause His mission just because people misunderstood Him.

That is the focus we need when gossip swirls around us. God did not call you to live for public approval or to protect a reputation. He called you to follow Him no matter what—through slander, gossip, and accusations—and to keep your heart anchored in His Word. So, the question becomes: *Will slander dictate the pace of your journey, or will you keep walking with your eyes fixed on Christ, not on critics?*

I know how hard that is. There have been times in life when I wanted to quit because I was exhausted, tired of rumors, and worn down by gossip. But each time I pulled back, the Spirit of God gently called me: *Don't stop. Don't let their words become your guide. My voice is still leading you.*

And He was and still is. When slander comes, and it will, you cannot afford to lose your focus on how others see you; your focus must remain on God and how He is transforming you. If Jesus did not let slander distract Him from the cross, then we cannot let it distract us from our mission.

So, keep going. Keep building, loving, and forgiving. Let your life preach louder than their words ever could. Ultimately, God does not call us to be admired; He calls us to a greater purpose.

WHEN SLANDER BECOMES FELLOWSHIP WITH CHRIST

Even when we know our purpose, the questions remain: "Why is this happening? Why are they allowed to speak about me like that?"

While those questions never came from Jesus, He never doubted the Father's justice or rushed to defend Himself in the court of public opinion. He did not need to because He knew who He *is*, why He came, and what it would cost Him.

And yet Jesus knows what it feels like to be misrepresented. He knows what it is like to stay silent, yet His heart was fixed on something greater than vindication. Slander did not catch Him off guard; it was woven into the path He chose.

He was called a deceiver. A blasphemer. A drunkard. A madman. A demon-possessed imposter. At His trial, false witnesses lined up to testify against Him. Matthew records it plainly: *"The chief priests, and elders, and all the council, sought false witness against Jesus... But found none: yea, though many false witnesses came, yet found they none"* (Matthew 26:59-60).

And still, *"Jesus held his peace"* (vs. 63). That silence embodied both strength and surrender. It was trust in the Father to write the final word, even as every human voice in the room shouted lies.

That changes how I see my own suffering. I now understand that Jesus has already walked this road. Every time we are falsely accused, abandoned by those we trusted, or judged unfairly, we are not merely suffering *like* Him, we are suffering *with* Him.

That means your tears are not wasted, your silence is not unnoticed, and your pain is not pointless. Jesus is closer than you think. A fellowship forms when we suffer as He did—a nearness, a clarity, a deeper dependence. And astonishingly, a beauty shines even through the ache of what you are enduring.

I have had nights where I lay awake, undone by someone's words, and yet, in that silence, I have felt Jesus draw near. When unjust words wound deeply, He does not stand far off. He comes close as our compassionate High Priest. Scripture assures us, *"For we have not an high priest which cannot be touched with the feeling of our infirmities..."* (Hebrews 4:15). He is touched. He is moved. He knows.

So, if the words have cut you... if you are weary of being misunderstood... if you have been judged, gossiped about, or left alone in the aftermath, know that Christ is not ashamed to draw near. He meets you in that place. He stands with the slandered. He comforts the falsely accused. And He holds close the one whose name has been dragged through the mud. Because His name was once dragged through the mud, yet He overcame.

MOVING FORWARD

Maybe the gossip still lingers in your ears. Maybe your heart still tightens when you walk into certain rooms, or when a notification pulls you back to memories you'd rather forget. Perhaps you still carry the sting of words that should never have been spoken.

If that is you, please know this: you are not the rumor being spread. You are not the caricature someone invented. You are beloved by God, fully known, and still chosen. His hands are still writing your story.

Slander can bruise your name, but it cannot touch your worth. It can shake your reputation, but it cannot uproot your calling. The same God who knit you together is also the same God who vindicates, restores, and rebuilds what others try to tear down.

You may never get the apology. You may never be truly understood. But that is not the end of your story. Healing is possible because Christ is greater than the wound. His truth speaks louder than the words spoken against you. His grace reaches deeper than the cut. His justice outlasts every false word.

So how do you move forward? Forgive—not because they deserve it, but because you refuse to stay shackled. Keep walking—not because the path is painless, but because God has more for you than the pit they dug. Choose prayer, not poison. Purpose, not pettiness. Mercy, not malice.

Speak life when others speak death. Live upright and faithful when others discredit you. When someone else's name comes up, especially someone who is struggling, you protect it. You do not need the whole story. God already knows, and that is enough. You choose grace, listen with discernment, and remember firsthand how words can wound, and how they can heal.

And that's the miracle, isn't it? That God can take a scar carved by words and turn it into wisdom. That He can take what was meant for evil and shape it into Christlikeness.

Let that be your testimony—not only that you survived the slander, but that you emerged softer, stronger, and more like Jesus. Let your voice, from this moment forward, be the one that heals, not harms… the one that builds, not breaks… the one that lifts, not tears down. Because in the end, your story isn't defined by what they said. It is defined by what *He* is still saying over you: "You are Mine. And I am not finished with you yet."

PART III

Finding Hope Beyond Suffering

16

WHEN YOU FEEL
LIKE GIVING UP

Burnout or emotional exhaustion does not always start with a tragedy. Sometimes the catalyst, the last straw, is toast burning in the morning or nobody saying thank you. It might be bills piling up or the car making that noise again. You are strong for everyone else until your own soul feels brittle. And then, somewhere between reheating coffee for the third time and scrolling past someone else's perfect life on social media, the words "I can't do this anymore" begin to surface. It is like something deep inside finally gave way, as if holding it in any longer might split you open.

You still go to church. You still smile. You still post Bible verses you're struggling to believe. But underneath it all is a part of you wondering if God sees how tightly you are holding on by a thread, how your prayers sound more like desperate hopes than certainties.

You want to be the strong, grateful one, the one who says, "God is good" and means it. But lately, your soul feels exhausted, as if it's running on fumes. And that moment when you say, "I'm fed up. I'm done," may actually be the first honest place you have stood in a long time, because you have stopped pretending. And that's where God meets you, right there, in that raw, honest place.

The Gospel was never about impressing God with how well you are holding everything together. It's about what He does when you admit you are falling apart. So, if your knees are buckling... if your prayers have turned into groans... if all you can manage is a faint whisper: "Jesus, help"—you're not failing. You are exactly where He meets people. Not to pull you out of the pain all at once, but to sit with you in it. To teach you what it means to rest in Christ. To walk with you slowly and honestly with a God who doesn't wait for you at the finish line, but steps into the mess and gently speaks, "I've got you."

LEARNING TO SIT AT CHRIST'S FEET

We are not good at being still. We fidget. Scroll aimlessly. Reach for distractions. We try to fix, move, numb—anything but sit quietly, especially when we are hurting. Silence feels heavy. Questions ring louder when we are not doing something about them. And yet... that is precisely where Jesus invites us: to come close, be still, and to simply rest in Him.

In Luke 10, Mary did something that seemed foolish to everyone around her. While Martha scrambled to prepare everything, Mary stopped. She sat right at Jesus' feet and simply listened. And Jesus honored her for it. He said, *"But one thing is needful: and Mary hath chosen that good part, which shall not be taken away from her"* (Luke 10:42).

While others scrambled to keep everything under control, Mary chose intimacy. When life feels like too much—when your thoughts race, your chest tightens, and you feel ready to break—this is your invitation to stop and simply be with Jesus. Sitting with Him is surrender. It's a posture of the heart that says, "I have nothing left... but I want to be near You.

It might look like collapsing into a chair and calling His name through tears. It might be lying face down on the floor with your Bible open, unsure what to pray. It might be walking slowly under the trees, mumbling, "I don't understand what You're doing, but I still want You."

This is about real presence with the One who does not demand eloquent prayers or spiritual performance, but simply invites you to come. Yet we often confuse motion with meaning. Some of the deepest healing happens when nothing moves except your heart, inching closer to His heart. *"Be still, and know that I am God..."* He tells us in Psalm 46:10.

This is a beautiful call for the overwhelmed. A wonderful invitation from the One who sees your spinning mind and says, "You do not have to fix this. Just stay near Me." Something many of us never learned in church: sitting with Jesus is not merely for the desperate moments; it is how your soul learns to breathe. If we only come to Him when we are falling apart, we miss the beauty of simply being with Him. Mary did not sit at His feet because she was falling apart; she sat because He was there. His presence was the peace her soul craved.

Maybe that's what you've been missing. We wait until everything falls apart before we come close. But what if peace does not wait until the storm passes? What if it begins when we slow down and sit with Jesus, just like Mary did?

PEACE THAT RISES IN THE STILLNESS

Slowing down matters so much because peace does not wait for life to calm down. It begins in the stillness. We often assume peace will arrive once the chaos subsides. But if you have ever sat in a quiet room with a noisy heart, you know that is not true. Peace does not wrap around you when every problem is solved, nor does it come from arranging life just right. It comes from something most of us never pause long enough to encounter. But when you finally stop striving and start surrendering, peace begins to awaken within you.

That is why sitting with Jesus matters so deeply. Not just because you are tired, but because you are thirsty. Your soul was never meant to survive on adrenaline and pressure; it was made to live in nearness to Christ. And when that nearness stops being your rescue plan and begins to shape your rhythm, you discover something richer than relief: His peace. As Isaiah 26:3 says, *"Thou wilt keep him in perfect peace, whose mind is stayed on thee: because he trusteth in thee."*

Notice it does not say "whose life is in order." It says, *"whose mind is stayed"*—anchored and fixed, not on your problems, but on God. Peace does not come when you finally gain control; it comes when your eyes lock onto Jesus, even if nothing else around you has changed.

But this is the part we struggle with: peace does not always feel like comforting calm at first. Sometimes it feels like silence, like nothing is happening. You sit at His feet, and instead of clarity, you get stillness. Instead of answers, you wait. Yet even then, something is happening.

Every time you choose not to run, not to numb, not to scroll or distract, something in you is being shaped. Even when you do not feel spiritual, you are training your soul to be resilient. You are letting His nearness do the healing.

Philippians 4:6-7 puts it this way: *"Be careful for nothing; but in every thing by prayer and supplication with thanksgiving let your requests be made known unto God. And the peace of God, which passeth all understanding, shall keep your hearts and minds through Christ Jesus."*

It does not say God's peace will solve your trouble. It says it will keep your heart and mind. Peace does not erase the chaos; it guards your heart from being swallowed by it. This kind of peace isn't built in shallow waters. It is forged in surrender, trust, and stillness. It is built on the repeated choice to return to His presence, again and again.

At first, you may not notice. But over time, something begins to shift. You do not react the same way. You are less frantic. You do not fall apart so quickly. The chaos hasn't vanished, but your soul has discovered something it hadn't known in a long time: rest. It feels like restoration from the inside out. And it all began the moment you stopped running, and dared to rest in the stillness.

WORSHIP IN THE MIDDLE OF THE STORM

Worship is one of the most beautiful mysteries of faith: the moments when it's hardest to sing are often the moments when it matters most. When your soul is heavy. When tears blur the page before you can finish the stanza. When lifting your voice feels like pretending. That is when worship stops being emotional and becomes an act of faith. Not because you feel inspired, but because deep in the ache, you know that God has not changed, and He is still worthy.

I have been there—aching, exhausted, and detached from anything that looked like praise. When my body was wracked with relentless spasms, there were days I could not even stand, let alone sing. I did not want to worship. I tried to argue with God. I wanted to give up.

But one day, desperate for something to hold onto, I cracked open my hymnbook, simply because I needed something steady when everything inside me was coming apart. And as I pushed out the words of the hymn, slowly, something began to stir. It was as if my soul was remembering what it was made for.

I began to worship. Not to escape the pain, but to resist it. Not because I understood God's plan, but because I refused to forget who He *is*. That is the power of praise. Worship does not erase suffering; it reframes it. It pulls your gaze from the storm to the One who commands it. It does not change the prison bars, but it changes your posture inside them.

That is exactly what we see in Acts 16. Paul and Silas, beaten and chained, did the unthinkable: from the despair of prison, they sang. *"And at midnight Paul and Silas prayed, and sang praises unto God: and the prisoners heard them"* (Acts 16:25).

They did not wait for their wounds to heal or for their chains to fall. They lifted their voices in the middle of it. And that shook the earth. Chains broke. Doors swung open. Hearts were changed.

That is what worship does in us, too. It loosens what grief has gripped. It unlocks doors inside us that we did not even know were shut. Because worship does not pretend pain is not there, it invites God into it. It is saying: "You are still good, even if this hurts. You are still righteous, even if I do not understand. You are still near, even when I do not feel You."

That kind of worship moves God's heart. So please do not wait until it feels easy. Sing when your throat is raw. Lift your hands when they shake. Cry out Christ's name when all you have left are tears. Even a broken hallelujah is still a hallelujah. And in that fragile place between pain and praise, something shifts, fear lifts, hope breathes again, and peace rises because you no longer face it alone.

THE PRACTICE OF GRATITUDE WHEN NOTHING FEELS GOOD

Gratitude feels effortless when life is going your way. When your body is strong, plans unfold neatly, and kindness surrounds you, it's natural to say, "Thank You, Lord."

But what happens when everything falls apart? What about when you are in the ER and no one can explain what's happening? Or when the dream you prayed and worked hard for crumbles in your hands? What does gratitude look like then?

This is the time when gratitude shifts from instinct to intention. It stops being a reflex and becomes a deliberate act of faith. It is written in Scripture: *"In every thing give thanks: for this is the will of God in Christ Jesus concerning you"* (1 Thessalonians 5:18).

Notice it does not say *for* everything. God never asks you to be thankful for betrayal, sickness, or injustice. But He invites you to look for Him *in* everything, even in what breaks your heart.

That changes how we see the dark days. It means you do not have to wait for the storm to pass to worship. You do not have to be healed before you say, "God, You're still good." His goodness is not tied to your comfort; it is anchored in His character. When life unravels, gratitude becomes a lifeline. It steadies your soul when despair threatens to pull you under.

In my past, there have been times when I have felt numb, drained, staring into silence, and unsure if anything would ever change. Prayer felt hollow. Hope felt out of reach. But in that heaviness, I began reaching for gratitude because it tethered me to the reality that God is near.

I began small. "Thank You for one more breath. Thank You for not letting go. Thank You for being here, even though I cannot feel You." Some days it came through clenched teeth. Other days through tears. But as I practiced gratitude during my dark days, the more I began to feel a sense of peace. It did not rush in; it rose like a slow tide, filling the space where despair once lived.

Gratitude does not erase grief. But it gives your soul room to breathe. It gently turns your attention from what is missing to what remains, from what you have lost to what can never be taken.

There is something deeply healing about speaking gratitude out loud; it changes the atmosphere around you. It pushes gloom to the edges. It confronts despair head-on. And even on days when everything feels heavy, it dares to say, "God is still good," not because life is easy, but because He has not changed.

Gratitude does not pretend everything is fine; it clings to God's faithfulness when nothing seems stable. When you choose it again and again, it becomes a doorway into peace rooted in surrender. No wonder

Psalm 100:4 urges us to *"Enter into his gates with thanksgiving, and into his courts with praise: be thankful unto him, and bless his name."* This was not written for easy days. It was written for weary hearts who need a way back into God's presence. Thanksgiving is that way.

So, start where you are. Write down your thanks. Speak them aloud. Notice the small mercies like the breath in your lungs, the blessings that linger, or the simple fact that you are still here. Give thanks for who He is, not just what He does.

Every time you choose gratitude in the midst of suffering, your soul finds deeper peace, not because the pain vanishes, but because God draws near just as He promised.

STRENGTH FOR THE NEXT STEP

Gratitude steadies your heart, and worship draws you near, but life does not pause. The world keeps spinning. And that is where faith takes its next breath. Eventually, the stillness ends and morning comes. The bills still show up. The memories still sting. And even after surrender, worship, and choosing gratitude, you still wake up in a world that has not changed.

But how do you move forward when you still feel fragile? How do you keep going when your body is tired, your soul still aches, and you are not sure you can take one more blow?

It feels a little like standing up after surgery. Everything is tender. Your balance is unsteady. Every moment takes effort. But just because you are not sprinting does not mean you are not healing. Sometimes progress is nothing more than a single step in the right direction—a step that still hurts, but is still a step.

Here is what I have learned while walking through these

seasons: you do not need to have it all figured out. You do not have to feel strong or certain. You simply need to trust God with the next small step. And sometimes that step looks incredibly ordinary: Replying to the message you have been avoiding. Opening your Bible when your mind feels foggy. Showing up at church even when you do not feel like singing. Letting someone pray for you when you would rather hide. Or taking a deep breath and choosing not to disappear.

Faith rarely looks impressive. It is almost never wrapped in clarity or joy. Sometimes it is walking with tears still on your cheeks. Sometimes it is simply doing the next right thing while God sees every step. Scripture says: *"Trust in the Lord with all thine heart; and lean not unto thine own understanding. In all thy ways acknowledge him, and he shall direct thy paths"* (Proverbs 3:5-6).

That verse does not promise a perfect roadmap. It promises guidance and presence.

The same God who met you in the stillness walks with you in the motion. He does not push you faster than you can bear. He is not impatient. He knows your wounds, your limits, and your pace. He leads gently.

I remember dragging myself outside for a late-night prayer walk close to midnight. I needed room to breathe and ask God some heavy questions. I was not trying to be spiritual; I simply needed God. And somewhere along that stretch of sidewalk, I realized He had been walking with me the whole time.

So, if you are wondering how to move forward when you still feel broken, you can. Not because you are strong, but because Christ is. You do not have to soar. You do not have to shine. You just have to keep moving, step by step, with Jesus beside you.

HOW TO KEEP GOING
WHEN YOU'RE READY TO QUIT

There are moments when giving up feels like the only option, but what most people never realize is this: the breaking point often sits right next to the beginning of change. Deep beneath the numbness and exhaustion, something sacred starts to rise. And when you have finally run out of strength, out of answers, and out of ways to fake your way forward, what remains is raw, honest, and ready for grace.

You may not feel like it now, but you were made for more than barely holding on. You were created to live with passion, courage, and purpose. Your feelings do not get the final word.

Even if you feel like only a shadow of who you once were, this wilderness you are walking through is not your identity. It is part of the journey, but not the definition of your life. You are still here because your story is not finished.

There is another way to think about the challenges you have been facing and the emotional fatigue that has been wearing you down. Maybe it feels so suffocating because the devil knows what God has placed inside you, and it rattles him. He knows the power of someone who's been to the edge, and still chooses Jesus. Heaven notices it too…which is why this is the very moment to lean in closer to Christ.

There were seasons when the weight was so overwhelming I truly wanted to give up: when lying down and never rising again felt easier than facing another day. But in those moments, I learned something I never expected: the answer wasn't trying harder, adding more spiritual tasks, or trying to fix myself. What kept me alive was staying close to Jesus.

Like me, you do not need a five-step plan to keep going. You do not need perfect clarity or certainty. What you need most is to stay close to the One who cares for you—your Creator who remains steady when everything else feels unsteady.

I used to picture faith as a steady climb upward. But more often, it feels like a wilderness. Some days we walk tall; other days we are just dragging our feet through the dust. Yet through it all, Jesus tenderly walks with us.

And maybe today, the next brave step isn't some big action. Perhaps it is letting the tears fall instead of being drowned by them. Maybe it is saying aloud, "I still believe," even when doubts linger. Perhaps it is calling a friend instead of shutting down. Maybe it is simply refusing to let despair write the ending. Whatever it looks like, today is not the end of your story.

The enemy wants you to believe your weakness disqualifies you. But Jesus looks at that very weakness and says, "This is where my grace runs deepest." Feeling fragile does not mean you are failing. You are not broken for needing rest. Being weary of the fight does not mean you are disappointing God. You are human.

The Gospel has never been about climbing your way to God. It has always been about God coming to you, stepping into your mess, sitting with you in the pain, and saying, "I'm not leaving."

So how do you keep going? You do not force it, and you do not fake it. You stay near to the One who is faithful. You walk through today. You let tomorrow come when it comes. And you trust that even when your strength is gone, He is still holding you.

Maybe this season is not about doing something big for God. Perhaps it is about discovering how deeply you are loved by Him, even when you have nothing left to give. So, if your hands are trembling... if your eyes are heavy... if your prayers feel scattered... stay. Jesus is here, and He has not changed.

You may feel like giving up. But He has never given up on you. God knew we would face moments like these. That is why He gave us these words in 2 Corinthians 4:8-9, 16 to cling to:

"We are troubled on every side, yet not distressed; we are perplexed, but not in despair; Persecuted, but not forsaken; cast down, but not destroyed...For which cause we faint not; but though our outward man perish, yet the inward man is renewed day by day."

That is your lifeline. Even in the unraveling... He is still renewing you.

---- **17** ----

THE HIDDEN GIFT IN SUFFERING

Suffering—a challenging topic none of us want to dwell on, yet one we all eventually face. It barges into life like an unwelcome guest, knocking things over as it comes. It disrupts your plans, steals your sleep, and rearranges your days. And no matter how many times you pray, it rarely leaves when you ask it to. It lingers, and it is demanding.

But there is a paradox hidden in the jagged hands of suffering, carrying a gift. I would not have believed it either until I found myself holding it. It is not a gift anyone asks for. It is not the one you hoped would come. Yet for reasons we cannot fully understand, God allows it in order to remake us.

If you have ever walked through deep suffering, you know this is not just hopeful talk. It is real. Your appetite shifts. Sleep becomes nonexistent. Laughter dwindles. You sit in a room full of people, feeling unseen, a shell of your former self. The concerns that once felt urgent suddenly lose their grip. And painfully, the life you knew begins to blur. In its place… someone new gradually starts to emerge. The pain has not left, but neither has God. And His presence begins to matter in ways you never imagined it could.

I once believed suffering only hardened people, making them bitter, closed off, and broken. And truthfully, I have been tempted more than once to stay angry, to blame God, to give up. But I have learned something in the fires: God never wastes affliction. He uses it to burn away what is shallow, self-made, and temporary. And what remains is someone truer, gentler, stronger, and closer to His heart.

So, this is not about "getting over" your suffering. It is about what it can become if you let it. If you give God access to your pain, He can do what no friend, no pastor, no therapist ever could— transform you from the inside out.

You may not feel it yet. But that ache, that crushing weight you carry, may be offering you a gift. A peculiar gift, yes, but one that can lead you into the deepest kind of transformation.

WHAT SUFFERING STRIPS AWAY

Suffering digs deep into our pride, our identity, and our sense of control. It strips away the things we did not even know we leaned on and pieces of who we thought we were.

I know this because there were times when it felt as though God was peeling me back, layer by layer. I was losing comfort, confidence, certainty, and the plans I had carefully built. I felt like I was falling apart.

One of the hardest blows came in mid-2023, when I had to leave El Salvador, a nation I deeply love, where I had poured my heart into young people trapped in gang violence and hard realities. I had thrown myself into that work. But with political shifts and a sweeping government crackdown, the opportunities to serve shut down almost overnight. Everything I thought I was there to do vanished. I left with the pang of failure pressing hard in my chest, unsure whether I would ever return.

But grace has a way of gifting us opportunities we cannot see in the moment. Eighteen months later, God provided and allowed me to return to El Salvador to do more work there.

Looking back now, I realize that I was not falling apart; I was being undone, which is not the same as being destroyed. When God removes something, it is to reveal, to cleanse, to bring into the light what is real and lasting. But in the moment, it feels brutal. It feels like everything you built is being torn down. Maybe that is the point.

Sometimes we are stripped of the illusion of control. Other times, it is the pressure to be strong for everyone else. Or it may be the belief that our worth comes from being useful, visible, or successful. When all of that falls away, we are left with the one truth that can never be taken: "God, I have nothing left but You. If I'm going to keep going, it will have to be You."

That is the moment when transformation begins. Not when we are strong. Not when we have solved the puzzle. But when the scaffolding of our lives collapses and we find ourselves bare, weak, emptied... and still deeply loved. That is where God starts building again. Not the version of us we used to be, but the one He has been shaping all along.

THE SLOW BECOMING

No one tells you how unhurried it will be. You expect to bounce back once the worst has passed. Regain your strength. Find your joy again. Maybe even return to the life you once knew. But suffering does not work that way. Neither does healing. Neither does becoming.

Transformation rarely looks like fire falling from the sky or a dramatic before-and-after photo. More often, it takes the shape of slow, unremarkable days. Days when you keep showing up and trusting, even when nothing seems to be changing, because beneath the surface God is doing what you cannot see.

I remember one of those periods within my own life. I was going to church, praying, and doing everything I thought I was supposed to do, but inside, I felt empty. I was not angry at God. I just was not close. I could not feel much of anything. At the time, I was sleeping on friends' couches, unsure what to do next. I prayed with desperation, but nothing seemed to change. No open doors. No dramatic provision. And it humbled me because I began to wonder if God would show up for me.

Looking back now, I realize that God was using that time to soften me. My heart began to change when my prayers shifted from shallow requests for instant relief to a more resounding cry to know Him. That is when I stopped clinging to a version of myself, I thought I should be, and began yielding to the one He was patiently shaping me into. It did not happen overnight. But it happened. One surrender at a time.

This is the pattern we see throughout Scripture. Moses spent forty years in the back end of the desert before God raised him up. It was not because he was forgotten, but because he was being formed. David was anointed king, then sent back to the sheepfold and later into exile; not because he was disqualified, but because he was being trained. Even Jesus spent thirty years in quiet submission before stepping into public ministry, waiting, growing, and learning obedience. Each one waited because God was establishing them for His appointed time.

We live in a world obsessed with quick change and instant results. Yet in the Kingdom of God, transformation is almost always unhurried. God delights to take His time. And He is never late. That is why Paul's reminder to the Galatians still matters: *"And let us not be weary in well doing: for in due season we shall reap, if we faint not"* (Galatians 6:9). That *"due season"* may not arrive when we hope for, but it always comes when God knows you are ready.

So, if you find yourself wondering why you are still stuck, why you are not "better" by now, why healing feels like it is taking forever, I want you to know that slow is not failure. It often means something deep is happening that cannot be rushed. God is working beneath the surface where no one else can see.

It may not look like progress. You may still feel weary. Still hurting. Still walking through fog. But do not mistake delay for denial. The becoming is happening. Even here. Even now.

WHAT THE FIRE REVEALS

There is something suffering reveals that nothing else can. God allows the fire of hardship to expose the desires beneath the surface and reveal whether we truly long for Him or if all we are looking for is relief.

It's a hard truth to face. But if you have endured intense suffering, you know it is real. Suffering burns away the surface layers of our faith. It leaves no room for performance or pretending. Suddenly, questions rise you never imagined asking: *Do I want God... or just His blessings?*

Most of us assume we are basically good—moral, God-fearing, deserving of something better than what we have. We may not say it aloud, but we live as if we do. We live as though God owes us, expecting Him to fix what is broken, bless our plans, and make life work as we intend. And when He doesn't, when suffering comes, we feel blindsided and even betrayed. But the fire was never meant to betray us; it was meant to reveal what is true about God, and about us.

I did not realize how much of my life had been built on comfort and ambition until they were gone. And if we are honest, many of us live the same way. We are driven by dreams, goals, and comfort, seldom pausing to ask the deeper questions: *What does God want? Why does God have me alive today?*

The truth is, we were not created to build a life for ourselves. We were created to know God: to enjoy Him and walk in fellowship with Him. That is the very reason He made us. But love cannot be coerced. That is the reason God gives us the freedom to choose. And one of the clearest places that choice is revealed... is in suffering.

Because when everything is stripped away, when the future is uncertain, and when the blessings feel far, we are confronted with the deepest question of all: What do we want most? God? Or escape? This is where the true intent of the heart is revealed.

In the book of Ruth, Naomi's story gives us a glimpse. After losing her husband and sons, she did not just grieve; she grew bitter. *"The Almighty hath dealt very bitterly with me,"* she said. Yet, even in her sorrow, God's faithfulness held her. And beside her was Ruth, who had lost much too, but responded differently. Her loss stirred a deeper longing for God Himself. Naomi pulled away. Ruth leaned in. And both were revealed.

For some, suffering reveals rebellion: a craving for control, a refusal to trust God's way. They harden and walk away. But for others, the fire awakens a different hunger for God Himself, a longing that suffering did not destroy but deepened. And that is where we begin to see: *I was made for more than this life. I was made for God.*

Suffering uncovers our true intentions and gives us the chance to choose again. To say through tears, through silence, through trembling hands: *"Lord, I still want You. Even now. You are enough."*

Don't get me wrong, this is not an easy place to reach. But when you do, you discover that you were made for more than survival; you were made for intimacy with God Himself.

TRANSFORMED TO TRANSFORM

When God transforms you, it is never solely for you. The comfort He pours into your wounds is meant to spill over. To become a stream of hope for someone else sitting in the dark, wondering if healing is even possible.

For a long time, I thought the goal was simply to survive, to stagger through the storm and collapse on the other side, barely breathing. But God's aim is higher than that. He is not merely shaping survivors; He is forming servants. And the tool He uses is often our wounds.

I think of my late mentor's wife, Georgia Drake, one of the godliest women I have ever known. For nearly seventy years, she and her husband opened their home, training and encouraging countless people in ministry. Georgia radiated joy and wisdom, even as her body suffered. In her later years, she lost her sense of taste, along with many other ailments. Eating became miserable to her, "like chewing sandpaper," she once said. But if you sat at her table, you never would have known. She still welcomed guests with laughter, grace, and warmth that could not be dimmed.

Some of the most Christlike people I have ever met were not the ones with the biggest platforms or the flashiest stories. They were the ones who walked through dark valleys, felt the crushing weight of sorrow, and came out softer and more gracious. They knew how to sit with the broken, not because they had all the answers, but because they remembered the loneliness of not having any. They had learned to weep with those who mourn because they still carried the memory of their own sorrows.

There is a kind of authority that can only be born from walking through fire with God, allowing that suffering to shape you. To strip away pretense. To make you tender and genuine.

This is what Paul meant when he wrote, *"[God] comforteth us in all our tribulation, that we may be able to comfort them which are in any trouble..."* (2 Corinthians 1:4). The healing God works within you becomes the medicine you now hold for others. Sometimes it is a word. Sometimes it is simply a hug. Sometimes it is the quiet grace of sitting beside someone in their grief. You do not need a title or to play a superhero, ready to save the day. What qualifies you is the scars that have been touched by Jesus.

And what's beautiful is that God does not wait until you are completely healed before using you. Some of the most powerful ministries I have ever witnessed have come from people who are still limping, learning to trust, and still in the midst of their own healing. It is not your strength that opens the door; it is your surrender. It is your willingness to pray, "Lord, if You can use this mess for Your glory, here I am."

Your story and your scars matter because they help someone else realize they are not alone. So do not wait for the storm to pass before you let God use your life. Even now, you can be a vessel of His comfort by being present, loving gently, and speaking honestly about where you have been and how God met you there. Carry the heart of Christ into another person's pain. Your suffering does not disqualify you. It is part of your commission.

STILL BECOMING, STILL BELONGING

There will be days when growth feels evident, and others when it feels you are slipping backward. Transformation is not a straight line; it is a journey marked by setbacks and progress. Yet, in every step forward and every stumble, grace is present, meeting you at every high and low, guiding and sustaining you.

If you are anything like me, there are days you wonder if you'll ever "arrive." Days when the old pain resurfaces. When a wave of grief or pain returns uninvited. When the accusing voices insist, "You should be past this by now."

Let me encourage you that becoming is a lifelong journey. There is no deadline on healing. No expiration date on grief. And needing Jesus every hour is not a weakness; it is the essence of faith. You may feel behind, but God still calls you beloved. You may feel stuck, but He sees you being shaped. You may feel like you are not doing enough, but He delights simply in your nearness to Him.

The beauty of it all is this journey is preparing you for eternity. Every choice of surrender, every act of faith, every prayer in the dark, every trembling "yes" to God is forming something eternal in you, something that will never be lost.

So do not despise the uneventful days. Do not condemn yourself for the wounds that still linger. Do not believe the lie that your story is over just because you are still healing. You are still becoming, but you already belong. One day, whether here or in Heaven, you will see it all. You will understand why the walls gave way, and why the silence stretched long, why the breaking felt so final. And I believe when you look back, it won't be with bitterness, but with gratitude. What you thought was a collapse was really Him at work, building. God was laying a foundation that reaches into eternity.

18

PITFALLS ALONG THE WAY

There is a curious hush that settles over the world in the hours before dawn. The clock ticks. Yet night lingers—slow, heavy, unhurried. And if you have ever suffered, you know that life begins to feel the same, like an endless night of the soul, waiting for a dawn that never comes. You lie awake staring at the ceiling, wondering if this heaviness will ever lift. If anyone sees you. If anyone understands. If anyone can reach you through this oppressive night.

Suffering has a way of distorting time. It stretches the minutes, blurs the days, until everything feels like one endless despair you cannot escape. And when suffering lingers, it does more than hurt—it tempts. It draws us toward quick fixes and false comforts—anything to dull the yearning, even for a moment. I have seen it. I have felt it. And if we are not careful, we will take the bait. We will run to what promises relief but delivers chains. And before we realize it, we are more worn down than before.

I would not be a friend to you if I skipped this part of suffering.

There is a danger in pain—it can pull you off course. It tells you to numb out, to escape, to give up. But you do not have to. You can recognize the traps. You can resist them. And by God's grace, you can choose a better path.

So, what are these pitfalls that suffering puts in our way? Let's walk through them together.

THE TEMPTATION TO ESCAPE

One of the first lies pain presses into your mind is: *You have to get out. Just make it stop. Whatever it takes.* And for many of us, that becomes the obsession. We scramble to find anything to dull the ache. At first, it does not look like rebellion. It may look like resilience or productivity.

For some, the instinct is to bury the discomfort under a mountain of activity. Fill every spare moment with distraction. Pour yourself into long hours at work, overload your calendar, or chase one project after another. On the surface, it looks admirable. The world applauds the overachiever who sacrifices rest in the name of discipline, ambition, or success. But deep down, we know what is really going on. We are not working; we are fleeing. We are afraid of what might rise to the surface if we ever sit still. We call it coping. But often, it's just hiding.

I've done that. Stayed busy just to avoid tension in my life. I told myself I was being productive. Responsible. Even faithful. But beneath all the motion, I was avoiding what I did not want to face. I did not want to sit still long enough to hear what the distress had to say.

Others might take a darker detour, seeking relief by spiraling into destructive activities. Reaching for alcohol. Gambling. Promiscuity. Overspending. Overeating. These escapes offer a flicker of relief and a fleeting, false calm. But when the high fades and the numbness wears off, the pain is there. Heavier now, burdened by regret. The same hollow strain returns, thirstier than ever.

Then there are those who chase the rush: the next thrill, the next trip, or the next wave of excitement. And for a moment, it seems to work. You feel alive again. Distracted. But it never lasts, does it? When the moment ends and the noise dies down, the emptiness is still there, unhealed. What began as an escape soon becomes a restless cycle that can be difficult to break.

The truth is, all these escapes share the same flaw: they offer temporary silence and not real healing. They are like pressing an ice pack against a broken bone; it numbs, but it never restores. The longer we avoid addressing what is broken, the deeper the fracture becomes.

The prophet Isaiah once delivered God's words to a restless people: *"In returning and rest shall ye be saved; in quietness and in confidence shall be your strength: and ye would not"* (Isaiah 30:15). That last phrase cuts deep—*"and ye would not."* God offered rest, peace, and wholeness. But His people chose distraction, noise, and motion.

Isn't that us too? We chase relief when what we truly need is God's presence. We stay busy when what we desperately need is rest in Christ. But what if you did not run? What if you let the heartache surface? What if you paused long enough to entrust your struggle to

God, "Lord, I don't want to escape. I want to heal"? This is where the real journey begins. Not when the sadness disappears, but when you stop trying to outrun it.

DANGER OF BITTERNESS, ISOLATION, AND NUMBING

Not everyone runs outward when they suffer. Some of us turn inward, and it can be just as dangerous.

Perhaps your pain has begun to harden. You are not just hurting anymore; bitterness or resentment has begun to settle in. You pull back from the people who love you. Maybe you are even pulling back from God, not intentionally, but quietly, slowly. You may never say it out loud, but the question echoes inside: *Why me? Why would God let this happen?*

I have felt this too while sitting in the stillness, replaying the same questions, and searching for answers that never came. Bitterness does not crash in all at once. It creeps in until one day you realize you have built walls of iron. Not just to protect yourself, but to keep everyone else out.

You stop replying to messages. You keep your distance at church. You avoid the people who might ask how you are *really* doing because deep down, you do not want to answer. It feels safer that way. But it is not. It is lonelier.

From the outside, bitterness may look like wisdom or self-protection, but in reality, it is a slow poison. It does not shield your heart; it closes it. And when you shut others out long enough, you often end up shutting God out, too.

Others do not grow bitter; they simply withdraw. When the pain feels too much to bear in public, they retreat. They vanish. Solitude feels like relief at first: no explanations, no expectations, no pressure to pretend. But isolation lies. It insists that no one cares. That you are a burden. That you are better off alone.

Scripture warns us: *"Through desire a man, having separated himself, seeketh and intermeddleth with all wisdom"* (Proverbs 18:1). In other words, isolation not only pulls us away from people; it warps our perspective. The longer we are alone, the louder the lies become. The darker the night feels.

Sometimes, instead of bitterness or withdrawal, we simply go numb. We shut down emotionally because we are exhausted. We have cried all the tears. Prayed all the prayers. And now we feel nothing. We go through the motions, smile when expected, say "I'm fine" while falling apart inside.

But numbness, too, does not heal. It might help us survive for a time, but it gradually deepens the wound. What we do not face, we cannot surrender; what we refuse to feel, we cannot offer to God.

I know firsthand that it feels easier to stay angry, distant, or numb. But these paths do not lead to peace. They only bury the pain deeper. Healing begins when we stop pretending it does not hurt. It starts the moment we open the door just a crack and let love in again. Even with a guarded heart, that one small sliver of honesty is where the light gets in. And that is all God needs to begin the mending.

THE HEALING PATH

Healing does not begin when the pain disappears. It starts the moment we stop pretending that we are fine, when we quit hiding behind busyness and fake smiles, and when we let the ache rise, daring to call out, "Here I am, Lord."

That is the turning point, because we have stopped striving and pursuing our own way. We have made room for God. And in that openness, He comes near. Patient. Gentle. Without shame.

God does not rush us. He does not scold us to get it together. He simply sits with us in the confusion, in the place we'd rather conceal, in the mess we cannot clean up on our own. Healing never comes by pushing sorrow away. It comes by letting Him into it. Sometimes the bravest prayer is the simplest one: "Jesus, I don't have the words. But I'm still here." And somehow, that is enough. He meets us in the silence. He mends us in the stillness. Slowly, gently, He begins mending together what we thought was beyond repair.

When we learn to trust God's Bible more than our feelings, our faith deepens. The pain may linger, but it no longer defines us. His grace begins to do what no distraction, no coping strategy, no earthly comfort ever could: restore.

Through grace, even suffering takes on a new shape. Not all at once, never neatly, but just enough to glimpse that this wilderness has purpose. That which once felt cruel can become sacred ground where intimacy with God takes root. And in time, we notice minor signs of life. Glimpses of hope. Tiny flickers of joy breaking through the numbness. Reminders that He has been working all along, even when we could not recognize it. That is the wonder of grace: not the removal of pain, but the nearness of God right in the midst of it.

GRACE IN WEAKNESS

God's grace often does not take the pain away. God's grace

transforms it into a place of communion. He takes the broken places in our lives and begins to redeem them, like a gardener tending scorched earth. He tills the soil, breathes life into what seemed dead, and what once felt like loss becomes fertile ground for something sacred.

The world is unsure of how to handle weakness. It demands, "Push through with sheer willpower. Try harder. Prove yourself. Be strong." But grace moves differently. It enters the moment we admit, "I can't fix this." It rushes in when our hands are empty and our strength has run out. That is where God does His tenderest work, not when we have figured it out, but when we have finally let go.

A few times in life, all I could do was crumble. In those moments, I expected God to shake His head and turn away. But instead, I found Him nearer than ever. He was not impatient or disappointed. He did not demand that I stand tall. He simply met me in the heap on the floor and held me there.

Jesus knew this pain too. He came as a man of sorrows, a Saviour who wept and suffered. He knows what it is like to feel misunderstood, exhausted, and poured out. He does not merely sympathize; He steps into our misery with us. And in that vulnerable, surrendered space where we stop pretending and performing, His strength becomes real.

Isaiah offers this promise, one that has comforted me countless times: *"He giveth power to the faint; and to them that have no might he increaseth strength"* (Isaiah 40:29). That is the hope we cling to when God breathes strength into our collapse. That is both survival *and* grace.

When we trust Him in our weakness, something begins to grow within us where faith matures and our lives are changed.

TWO RESPONSES TO PAIN: DAVID AND SAUL

We have already seen glimpses of David's life in the betrayals, the losses, and the grief. But one of David's most remarkable qualities was how he responded to that suffering. He kept returning to God, even after failure, even after sin. His life was far from perfect, but his heart never stopped reaching for the Lord.

The Psalms are filled with these returns as raw, unfiltered prayers poured out in the wake of anguish. David did not pretend to be strong or try to impress anyone. But he didn't shut God out, either. He let the yearning turn into an honest conversation with God. That is what made him a man after God's own heart. Though flawed, he kept coming back, no matter how broken he felt.

Now, contrast that with Saul, who also had his challenges. He knew fear and bore the weight of leadership, failure, and insecurity. Rather than allowing it to humble him, he let it harden his heart. Rather than drawing near to God, he clung ever tighter to control. In God's silence, he sought guidance from a medium, proof of how far his heart had drifted.

Saul did not start that way. He began with promise. He was chosen, anointed, and hopeful. But a heart unwilling to yield to God eventually collapses under strain. His downfall was gradual; it was the slow erosion of trust. He never let God into the pain.

That is what sets David and Saul apart. Both were flawed, and both suffered. One ran toward God with a humble heart; the other pulled away, hiding behind walls of pride and fear. And that contrast is both a warning and an invitation for us today. Suffering will come. Pressure will mount. Fear will press in. However, how we respond, whether we lean in or pull away, can change everything.

So, let me ask you gently: in your season of struggle, are you more like David or Saul? Are you turning toward God or have you begun to close off and harden, seeking other voices when His feels distant? You are not condemned for your mourning. But you *are* invited to bring it somewhere. Do not let your suffering drive you further into silence or self-reliance. Let it drive you toward the One who already knows every corner of your heart.

ENCOURAGEMENT IN TESTIMONY

Over the years, there were times when the weight I carried felt unbearable, and I found myself tempted to numb it all—to distract myself, to flee, to withdraw—because in those moments, it felt like the only way to breathe. But I have also known what it is to bring that emptiness to Christ, and find Him waiting with open arms.

Every time I turned to Jesus, whether in a flood of tears or a cry of desperation, He met me. He did not always change my circumstances. But He changed *me* in the midst of them. He taught me that healing does not come through willpower. It comes from letting go. From relying on His strength instead of my own.

So, if you feel stuck, perhaps trapped in the same mistakes or circling the same struggles, I want you to know that there is a way forward. You do not have to stay buried beneath the weight. You do not have to keep running from hurt. God sees it. He sees you. And He is not distant; He is inviting you right into His presence.

Yes, there will be seasons when no human help is available, but God allows it so we will discover the only Help who never fails.

Getting unstuck begins with surrender. By laying your burdens down with honesty. It begins when you stop trying to escape the despair and start handing it to the One who already carried it all.

Wholeness is not found by pretending we are fine. It comes when we bring our questions, fears, and exhaustion to Jesus. And as we walk with Him, even when progress feels slow, and we stumble, we begin to see that He is our hope and our healer. Our refuge. Our steady joy.

THE INVITATION OF CHRIST

Jesus extended this invitation, *"Come unto me, all ye that labour and are heavy laden, and I will give you rest"* (Matthew 11:28).

These words were spoken openly to a crowd in Galilee, ordinary men and women living under Roman rule. These were people worn down by years of physical hardship, emotional exhaustion, and religious strain. Some had already hardened their hearts. Others were quietly breaking beneath the surface. And to all of them—not just the religious, but those struggling under the weight of guilt, shame, and fear—Jesus offered something radically different: an invitation to rest. Real rest. The kind that does not come from trying harder but from coming closer; a nearness to God that no system or self-effort could ever produce.

Jesus was not simply offering comfort. He was offering Himself: a Saviour who knows what it means to suffer. One who did not sidestep misery but stepped straight into it for us, so that we could find peace.

Jesus knows the depth of what you are feeling and carrying—

the pressure, the grief, the fears you haven't dared to say out loud. He is not asking you to fix it or figure it all out. He is just asking you to come to Him.

So, if you find yourself today numbing, blaming, withdrawing, or reaching for distractions that never satisfy, pause. Look up. Christ is still there, still calling to you. He may not remove the distress overnight. But He will walk with you through it step by step with grace that holds and strength that never runs out.

When we surrender our hurts to Him, Jesus does not allow them to go unused. He uses them to transform us slowly and deeply. The same weight that once crushed us becomes the place where God teaches us to breathe again, to trust again, and to live again.

You do not have to be perfect or have it all together. You just need to come to Christ with honesty, openness, and a willing heart. This is where healing begins.

So do not keep running. Do not let the anguish push you deeper into distraction or despair. Christ's invitation still stands, and it is gentle, open anytime, and waiting for you to accept. Bring all of it, just as it is. Let Him hold what you cannot carry anymore. Let Him restore what you thought was too far gone because you are not abandoned. God is faithful. Your suffering will not be wasted. In Christ, even the darkest valleys can become the beginning of your brightest hope.

19

GOD'S ULTIMATE VICTORY

Have you ever stood at the edge of something that felt too big to make sense of? A moment so heavy it steals your breath and leaves you wondering if you will make it through.

Now imagine this: you are standing on a cliff overlooking a restless ocean. Wind is whipping around you. Waves crashing against the rocks below. Rain cutting across your face. Everything feels out of control. And yet... inside, there is a calm and quiet confidence. You know this storm will not last forever. You cannot explain it, but somehow, you are certain this is not the end.

That is a glimpse of what it feels like to cling to God's victory in the very heart of suffering. When grief crashes over you and despair shouts louder than truth, there is still an anchor that cannot be moved. God's victory stands firm when your world falls apart. His faithfulness does not waver when everything else gives way.

Maybe you have been at the edge of that cliff yourself—a hospital waiting room, a police station, or lying awake at 3 a.m., begging God to make it stop. And all you had left was faith.

Here is the truth: God's victory did not begin with your hardship, and it did not begin with your story. It began before time ever breathed its first moment—when the Ancient of Days, full of mercy and wisdom, made the way through His Son. And the beauty is that this victory is present right here, in your grief, your confusion, and your weakness. Christ's triumph still holds. Nothing in Heaven needed to be reclaimed. But you did, and He won you fully.

So how do we live in that victory, even while we are still bleeding? Let's walk into that together.

CHRIST'S SUFFERING: OUR PATH TO REDEMPTION

God's victory did not show up the way we would have written it. It did not arrive on chariots. It did not blaze through the skies with fire. It did not overthrow Rome or silence every critic in a single breath. No, God's victory came in the most unexpected way: through weakness and bloodied skin in the body of the Saviour, who chose to suffer because no other path could show us just how deep His love goes.

Jesus could have entered the world with thunderous applause and glory. He could have summoned angels or commanded kings. But instead, He chose the womb of a teenage virgin. He came wrapped in human fragility, clothed in scandal, and veiled in mystery. The *Word became flesh*, and from the very beginning, He allowed Himself to be misunderstood.

He was not born in a palace. There was no crown or royal welcome; only the cold, crude shadows of a stable. The first breath of air he breathed smelled of livestock. The first bed He lay in was a feeding trough. And the descent continued. As a toddler, Jesus became a refugee. His family fled to Egypt, escaping Herod's rage and slaughter. When they finally returned two years later, He was not raised in Jerusalem or a respectable town. He grew up in Nazareth, a town so dismissed that people scoffed, *"Can there any good thing come out of Nazareth?"* (John 1:46).

People gossiped. They twisted the story of His mother's pregnancy. They speculated and whispered. After Joseph passed away, the rumors only grew louder. Jesus heard every word. He saw every sideways glance. He carried the weight of every insinuation. He knew the pain of being judged before He was ever truly known.

Jesus did not merely taste suffering; He lived in its chaos. Scripture says, *"Though he were a Son, yet learned he obedience by the things which he suffered"* (Hebrews 5:8). Suffering became the furnace where His humanity was fully revealed. He knew hunger. He knew exhaustion. He knew the grinding labor of a carpenter's life.

In Nazareth, He felt the weight of oppression through religious elitism, Roman domination, classism, and poverty. He knew what it felt like to be dismissed, overlooked, and ignored. And yet... He kept going.

He wept at gravesides, even though He knew resurrection was coming. He cried over Jerusalem, fully aware they would reject Him. He felt the sting of siblings who doubted Him. He endured slander, suspicion, and betrayal from the very people He came to rescue. And still, He did not stop there. He walked all the way to the cross. He became sin for us. He carried the penalty of our rebellion and the full weight of our shame, guilt, and judgment. He bore our filth so that His righteousness could clothe us.

In that sacred, agonizing moment, the Son who had always known perfect communion with the Father experienced separation. We will never grasp the depths of that agony. But we hear it in the silence between His words: *"My God... My God... why hast Thou forsaken Me?"*

Yet, Jesus chose to be forsaken because He would rather endure being forsaken from the Father for an afternoon than be without you for eternity. And even that was not the end. Death tried to chain Him. But it could not. The grave swallowed Him, but had to spit Him out. He rose so He could rewrite your story. He ascended into Heaven and now sits at the right hand of the Father as your Great High Priest. He still intercedes. Still understands. Still bears the scars—scars that still speak: You do not have to earn your victory. You get to live from it.

Jesus did not merely suffer for you; He suffered as you. He stepped into your condemnation. He bore what you could not. He conquered what would have crushed you. That is why sin no longer defines you. That is why shame has no claim over you. And that is why the pain you are walking through has already been overthrown by the One who defeated it completely.

So, the question is not, "Can I get through this?" The real question is, "Will I let Christ carry me through it?"

Will you keep clutching the fear, the hurt, the pride, the bitterness? Or will you finally take hold of the hand that has been reaching toward you since before you were born? You do not have to prove yourself. You do not have to bear this weight alone. Jesus has already carried it, and He has already won.

JESUS IS WITH US NOW

Let's be honest. Sometimes "victory in Jesus" does not feel very victorious. We know the phrase. We sing about it. We quote it. But when the diagnosis comes, or the phone call shatters your world, or the prayers go unanswered for the hundredth time, it can feel like that victory belongs to someone else—someone stronger or holier.

But the truth is that victory in Jesus does not mean your pain disappears. It does not mean life suddenly gets easier. However, it *does* mean you are not alone in it. And I do not mean that in the sentimental way, we often hear from pulpits. I mean it in the most literal way possible. Jesus is here right now. Not as an idea. Not figuratively. But as a living, breathing, present Saviour. The same Jesus who wept beside Mary. The same Jesus who touched the leper. The same Jesus who bled under Roman lashes, who hung between thieves, who cried, *"It is finished."* That Jesus lives in you this very moment.

He has not left you for a single second. You may feel forgotten. You may feel invisible. But He sees every piece of what you are walking through, and He is right there in the thick of it with you. He is in the room when your faith feels like it is slipping. He is near when your prayers feel empty. He is present when you wonder if you are still loved after everything.

He promised: *"I will never leave thee, nor forsake thee"* (Hebrews 13:5). Not just on the mountaintop. Not only when your worship feels strong. But especially in the wilderness when your heart grows heavy. Especially when you are falling apart. When all you have left is a faint plea: "Lord, help." That is when His nearness becomes the most tender.

He is not waiting for you to clean up before He comes near. He already came. And He is not going anywhere. Paul called it *"Christ in you, the hope of glory"* (Colossians 1:27). Think about that: Christ *in* you. Not beside. Not nearby. In. And one day soon, He will return in flesh and blood, in full, breathtaking majesty. The One who suffered will come back in glory. And when He does, the pain, the fear, and the losses will *not* get the final word. The shadows you have walked through will vanish in His light. The ache that weighs your soul will dissolve into joy so real that you will want to both shout and fall to your knees with a *hallelujah*.

But until that day comes... we wait. We walk through the valleys, and sometimes the wilderness. Psalm 23 calls it *"the valley of the shadow of death."* But pause—what does it actually mean? It is a phrase we often hear, but do we truly understand what it is saying about the way God walks with us through our darkest times? A shadow only exists because something real is nearby. But it is not the thing itself; it is the outline. The impression. That is what Jesus left for us.

He took the real thing, death itself, so all that remains for us is the shadow. The fire of judgment fell on Him. The weight of wrath crushed His whole being before the resurrection ever came. He endured the distance, the silence, and the separation from the Father so you would never have to.

And now, when you suffer, you do not face the wrathful furnace. You walk through the smoke with Someone who already survived the fire. Yes, the shadows are dark. Yes, they still make your spirit quake. But they cannot consume you. Jesus walks with you through both the smoke and the shadow.

And the promise of Heaven is not a vague comfort for

someday. It is what holds you steady now. It is a reminder that where you are headed is better than anything you have left behind. So, while you walk, remember Jesus is walking too. He is within you and beside you. He is holding you.

If today feels heavy—if the silence feels suffocating, if the valley feels endless—do not let go. Do not cling to a doctrine, cling to Christ. He is your Shepherd, your Friend, and your anchor in the storm. The ache you feel right now is not brushed aside or overlooked or too much for Him to carry. It matters to Him. He sees it. He feels it. And He is not going anywhere.

THE GLORY THAT AWAITS

There is a promise etched into every tear Christians shed: *This will not last forever.* The sorrow you are holding may feel endless, but it is not. We live between Eden and eternity. Between what was lost and what will one day be restored. We watch people we love die too soon. We hear diagnoses that steal our breath. We walk through heartbreaks and injustices that blindside us without warning. And some days, it is hard to imagine beauty ever rising from such ruin. But do not mistake delay for denial. God has not forgotten you.

Scripture is unflinching: beauty will rise from ashes, but glory is coming. And not a vague comfort, but a reality so wonderfully overwhelming, so personal, it will outshine every sorrow.

Romans 8:18 does not merely compare; it insists comparison is impossible: *"For I reckon that the sufferings of this present time are not worthy to be compared with the glory which shall be revealed in us."* Let that sink in.

It is not simply that Heaven will be better. It is that your suffering will not even be worth mentioning next to it. Take the worst moment, multiply it by a lifetime, and hold it against what is coming; and it will not even cast a shadow. Why? Because that glory is yours and will be revealed in you.

This is what we are waiting for: not just relief from pain, but the fullness of glory in you and around you. Not just an escape from sorrow, but the presence of the Saviour who walked every step with you. And on that day, you will not be asking why life was so hard because in His presence, the grief will no longer matter. Your eyes will not be searching for explanations. They will be fixed on Jesus Christ.

For now, we cling to that hope like a lighthouse in a storm. At times it feels faint, but it is always steady. But one day, you will not cling to it. You will step into it, breathe it in, wear it as a robe, and live in it like a child finally home. Revelation 21:4 gives us a glimpse too beautiful to rush past: *"And God shall wipe away all tears from their eyes; and there shall be no more death, neither sorrow, nor crying, neither shall there be any more pain: for the former things are passed away."*

Imagine no more hospitals, funerals, "we lost the baby," or "I'm sorry, it is terminal." No more lamentations. No more silent suffering. No more numbing just to survive.

The same hands pierced for your redemption will touch your cheeks and wipe away sorrow forever. Heaven is a place, yes, but the treasure is not golden streets or pearly gates. The treasure is the Lord Jesus Christ. He is the light of that city, the joy that fills its streets, the brilliance that draws every heart into worship.

When you finally see Jesus, you will understand that every pain had a purpose. Not because pain is good, but because God is better. And He used every tear, every setback, and every injustice to carve into you a deeper love for Him.

When you enter Heaven, you will laugh again, with the kind of joy that bubbles up from a soul finally free. You will not be a guest; you will be family. Jesus did not die merely to make you a citizen of paradise. He died to make you a child, a co-heir with Him in glory. Your view of life will shift. The questions that once haunted you will fade. The regrets that weighed you down will fall. And the years stolen from you? Restored, overflowing with joy that has no end.

That is what awaits you. Not just a new home, but a new heart. Not just a place, but a Presence that fills you to the core. You will not long for closure. You will not search for meaning. You will be swallowed up in joy. Breathing relief, wearing it like a crown. Everything empty will be filled with purpose. And you will finally know that nothing from your life, not even the pain, was wasted.

So, press on, beloved, because Heaven is real, and Jesus is waiting. And when you arrive Home, He will say, "You made it. I saw every step. I held every tear. And now… *You are Home*." And indeed, it will be Home, forever.

THE COMPASSION OF CHRIST

Most people think of compassion as an action Jesus *did*. But what if it is more than an action? What if compassion is simply who He is? Before there was sin to forgive or wounds to heal, compassion was already living in the heart of God.

We often overlook the fact that Jesus showed compassion before anyone asked for help. He wept at Lazarus' tomb before Mary and Martha spoke a word. He touched the leper before the man even dared to believe. He raised the widow's son in Nain without request, because she was too crushed to ask.

This reveals something profound: God does not wait to measure how deep your pain runs before He moves. He feels first. He acts first. He loves first. What kind of King does that? Only Jesus. Every step He has taken has been a step into our pain. He chose a womb before a throne, tired feet before glory, along with hunger, heartbreak, and betrayal—all before He ever asked us to follow.

That is not just compassion. That is grace walking ahead of you.

The humility in that is overwhelmingly breathtaking. He made our brokenness His own. He did not merely observe our grief; He absorbed it. At times, it crushed Him. Think of Gethsemane, where He sweated drops of blood under the weight of what was coming. This was love so profound that it broke His heart before the cross touched His body.

Have you ever loved someone so much that their grief made you physically sick? Jesus has for the whole world. And the stunning truth is that He still feels it.

We often speak of Jesus' compassion as if it were in the past tense. But Hebrews 4:15 does not say He understood our weaknesses. It says He is touched with the feeling of our infirmities. Present tense.

The risen Christ still remembers the taste of tears, the weight of a cross, and the sting of being called a devil. The scars He carries are His way of saying, *"I still see you. I still know."*

When you enter Heaven, His will be the only scars in sight. And in an instant, you will know that He understands everything you have been through. And He does not regret what it cost Him.

In Luke 12:37, Jesus says something breathtaking: in the Kingdom, He will gird Himself and serve us at the table. Think about that. The King of creation is still serving, stooping, and pouring out love with nail-pierced hands, even in Heaven.

He does not lay aside compassion when He puts on His crown. He is the Saviour waiting at the end of your long, weary road. And when you look into His eyes, you will finally know just how loved you have always been. For the King and Creator has never stopped feeling for you; His heart has been with you all along.

FACE TO FACE WITH OUR CREATOR

One day... it will all be behind you. Every tear you have cried, every ache you have felt in secret, and every storm that made you wonder if anyone cared—gone!

What lies ahead is more than relief and rest. It is the face of the One who knit you together before the world formed. The One who stood with you in rooms where no one else stood. The One who wept when you wept, who whispered peace into your storms you mistook for silence. You will see Him face-to-face.

Scripture says it plainly: *"For now we see through a glass, darkly; but then face to face..."* (1 Corinthians 13:12). You will stand before Him with nothing hidden or veiled, fully known, fully accepted, and fully loved by the One who carried you the whole way through.

And it will not just be peace you feel; it will be completion. Every unanswered question will lose its urgency. Every pain will dissolve into purpose. Every voice that ever told you that you were not enough will fall silent in the smile of His eyes. Because when you see Him, you will realize He was never ashamed of your doubts, your weaknesses, or the moments you feel apart. God does not think of you by your failures. As the psalmist wrote, *"For he knoweth our frame; he remembereth that we are dust"* (Psalm 103:14). And He loved you all the same.

Think of it: the same hands that flung galaxies into existence will reach out to hold your face in joy. The same voice that thundered over Mount Sinai will summon your name to welcome you Home. The One whose holiness once made mountains tremble and burn... will smile at you.

In that moment, you will not just be in Heaven. You will be *Home*. Because the One you have longed for will be there, wrapping eternity around you like a garment of glory. And suddenly, it will not matter that you limped across the finish line. It will not matter that you doubted, wrestled, or wandered because He was carrying you all along.

And here is something wonderful: You will not only finally know Him, but you will also finally know yourself. Paul writes, *"then shall I know even as also I am known"* (1 Corinthians 13:12). You will finally see what He has always seen when He looks at you: A beloved child—redeemed, restored, and radiant. A reflection of His beauty, formed through every hardship, now crowned in glory.

And He will wipe away every tear because you will not need them any longer; not even the happy ones. Absolute joy will be too full, too sacred, and too consuming for tears. His joy will fill every fiber of you like sunlight through stained glass, flooding your soul with every color and warmth.

That day is not far. And when you finally see Him, you will not ask, "Why did I suffer so long?" You will ask instead, "How did You love me so well through it all?"

It Is Enough!

So, when the journey feels long, do not forget what is waiting for you. Not just a throne, not just a crown, but the face of the One who has loved you since before time began. He is the victory. And soon... you will see Jesus face-to-face.

20

COMFORTING OTHERS...
AND YOURSELF

There is a kind of pain you can recognize without a word being spoken. It is in the woman at the pharmacy, clutching her prescription as if it were the last thread holding her together. It is in the teenager staring blankly out a bus window with his earbuds in, though no music is playing. It is in the elderly man who lingers after church because no one is waiting for him at home.

The world is full of silent suffering: pain that hides in plain sight. Despair that does not scream. Grief that does not show itself. Wounds hidden behind casual replies of, "I'm fine.

If you have truly walked through suffering, you begin to see it everywhere, in the tired eyes of others. You understand the ache of feeling invisible, the heaviness you carry that no one else seems to notice. And sometimes suffering gives you new sight, like a window cracked open to let in the light.

By now, you don't need anyone to explain pain to you. You

have lived it and grieved through it, and maybe even wrestled with God in the middle of it. After all you have endured, there is something deeper to consider: *What if your suffering was not only for you?*

What if the God who met you in the dark now wants to guide you into someone else's life, simply to walk beside them?

We often think of trials as private battles. But Scripture turns that upside down. Suffering becomes a platform, a ministry, even a calling to step back into the fire—not to relive your pain, but to help someone else going through their own.

I once heard someone say, "The greatest comfort you can give is the comfort you had to fight for." That stayed with me. Because when someone who has been there steps down into your darkness, their presence carries more credibility than any simple advice ever could. It is the gift of presence, and it is the heart of Jesus.

Helping others in their suffering is a hallmark of the Christian life. It becomes the natural outflow of a heart that has been broken, healed, and made willing again. It is how Christ lived. And it is how He calls us to live as well.

Until Heaven is our eternal Home, this is our assignment: to walk through this broken world with open eyes and open hands. See the hurting. Stay with the grieving. Stand with the weary. And in the same way God met us in our lowest moments, we now have the privilege of meeting others when they are barely holding on. Because love does that. It enters. It draws near. It walks beside the wounded and helps bear some of the burden.

THE COMFORT THAT MOVES THROUGH YOU

God's comfort is personal and always timely, specific, and

intentional. He steps into our pain with tenderness that words cannot capture. He knows how to speak peace into places we have never spoken aloud.

And His comfort is not meant to end with us. What He pours into our brokenness is meant to spill over into someone else's life. His mercy does not stop with us; it flows through us like living water meant for other thirsty souls.

This is how suffering becomes ministry. We are not only survivors; we become vessels, witnesses, and messengers of the same hope that once held us together when everything else was falling apart. That is what makes the church sacred. We gather as wounded healers— people who know what it feels like to fall apart and still find God faithful. The grace God pours into our wounds is never meant to stop with us. The grace we receive becomes the grace we extend to others.

Your pain may have felt like a private burden. But what if it was preparation? What if the wilderness you walked through is similar to the one someone else is stepping into, and you are the person God wants to meet them there?

When you have sat in the dark, you know how to sit with others still there. When you have questioned your worth, you know how to speak value into someone else's life. When God met you in your lowest moment, He was not only rescuing you, He was equipping you for this very purpose.

That is why, when I see someone struggling, I try to show up for them. One afternoon, I came across two men sitting on the curb— lost, hunched over, and despondent. I had some extra sandwiches, so I offered each of them one and gently said, "Jesus really does love you."

That was all it took. One of them, named Alberto, began to cry, softly at first, then uncontrollably. I sat with him on the sidewalk and shared a little of my story: how I had once known the loss of everything, and how Jesus did not just rescue me; He taught me lessons I still hold dear. That day, Alberto bowed his head and called on Christ to save him. All of that, simply because of a kind presence, empathy, and a sandwich.

Many people believe they must be fully healed before they can help others. But often, it is your weakness that becomes a tool for ministry. Your scars become the places where God's comfort turns into your calling. You do not need a platform to be useful. You do not need a degree to make a difference. You only need to share the comfort you have already received. Somewhere out there, someone is suffering in silence, wondering if anyone sees them; and maybe God wants to comfort them through you.

CHRIST CAME CLOSE

Jesus never healed at arm's length. He did not shout truth across the crowd, keeping Himself untouched by people's pain. He drew near. He let the lepers come when no one else dared. He touched the untouchables. He noticed the trembling woman reaching for His robe. And when she touched Him in desperation, He did not recoil. He turned toward her.

That is the kind of Saviour we have. Not one who merely observes suffering, but one who embraces it with us.

Jesus did not minister with polished speeches or rehearsed lines. He ministered with presence and warmth, with eyes that locked onto people long forgotten by the world. His love was messy, personal, and full of compassion. He walked among the sick. He knelt with the grieving. He stopped for the outcast. Never once did He treat someone's suffering as an inconvenience.

And that is the picture of ministry He left us. Not a ministry of words, but of nearness. Not a performance, but a presence. Not a rescue mission that keeps our hands clean, but a love willing to get dirt under the fingernails.

Too often, we try to help in ways that keep us safe. We text a verse, leave a comment, shoot up a quick prayer. Sometimes those attempts are helpful. But there is a difference between offering help and offering yourself. Jesus chose the harder way. He showed up. He made room. He carried the burden. And if we claim to follow Him, how can we do any less?

There are people in your life right now who do not need your advice. They need your presence. They do not need a theology lesson; they need a steady friend. They do not need a rescue plan; they need someone who will sit with them in the ashes and not flinch. Because sometimes the most powerful promise you can offer is, "I'm not leaving."

We all know the difference between someone who throws words at our pain and someone who chooses to *stay* with us in it. That is the difference between information and incarnation. Between sympathy and *Emmanuel*, meaning *God with us*.

To minister like Christ means slowing down long enough to really see people. It means letting your heart be pierced by someone else's sorrow. It means saying "yes" to the inconvenience of love. And yes—it will cost you. It will cost you your time, your comfort, and energy. Sometimes, it can even cost you your sense of safety, cleanliness, or control. But it is in that place of sacrifice that you reflect Jesus most clearly. Because He did not avoid our pain. He entered it head-on, with arms stretched wide and nails through His flesh. And now, He turns to us and says, *"Follow Me."*

THE SACRIFICE THAT TRANSFORMS

It is easy to feel like you have done your part when you say, "I'm praying for you."

It is easy to send a verse, offer a smile, or type out a kind comment. Those gestures are not meaningless, but love that transforms rarely stays at a distance. True ministry is not tidy. It shows up in the middle of the mess. It walks into broken homes, jail cells, nursing homes, and broken hearts—and refuses to look away.

Helping someone who is suffering almost always interrupts your day. You may lose sleep or have to cancel plans you had for the evening. It may mean listening when you are already drained or sitting with someone who cannot put their pain into words.

I learned that firsthand back in my twenties, when I passed a woman begging on the street. Her clothes were dirty, and her face was weary. I knew I could not fix everything. Still, I felt prompted to do more than hand her a few dollars. A small restaurant was nearby, so I asked, "Would you like to have lunch with me?" Her eyes widened, and she agreed.

We sat together as she shared some of her story. Before we parted, I told her I was sorry I could not do more, but I wanted her to know that not everyone is too busy or too cold to notice. There are people who care.

That moment did not change the course of her life. But it

reminded me that true ministry often begins in small, unplanned acts of compassion. It starts in the ordinary, in the interruption, and in the willingness to slow down and be present. Sometimes, that is precisely where God begins to call you on a deeper level. He never promised that comforting others would be convenient, but He did promise it would be worth it.

When you step into someone else's troubles, you are not just meeting a need, you are meeting Christ: The One who said, *"Inasmuch as ye have done it unto one of the least of these... ye have done it unto me"* (Matthew 25:40). When you love someone in their lowest moment, you are standing on sacred ground.

One of the beautiful aspects of this is that while you are pouring yourself out, God is quietly filling you. While you sacrifice comfort, He softens your heart. While you stoop to carry another's burden, He bends and molds you. The paradox of ministry is that it transforms both the one being helped and the helper.

When you give your time, your attention, your presence, your tears... you are offering something the world cannot counterfeit. You are becoming a reflection of Christ in a world that barely remembers His name. And thankfully, you do not have to be whole to walk with someone in their pain. You just have to be willing.

God does not ask for polished perfection; He asks for availability. He uses the humble, the downtrodden, and those who limp a little when they walk. They know the way down, and they remember how it felt when someone came and sat beside them.

So, bring what you have: a quiet word, a tear, an open hand, a listening ear. That is how ministry begins. Because when you enter someone's suffering, you are offering them Christ. And Christ is always enough.

PRESENCE IN A DETACHED WORLD

The kind of presence Christ modeled is not always easy to offer, especially in our modern world. We are more "connected" than ever, and yet more disconnected than ever before.

You can message someone across the globe in a split second. Scroll through hundreds of faces in minutes. Watch headlines about wars, disasters, and heartbreak, all while lying comfortably in bed. You can even type "Praying for you" while binge-watching a show. But none of that means we are truly present.

We confuse proximity to information with proximity to people; they are not the same. Jesus did not scroll past the hurting. He did not stay at a safe distance and say, "Be warmed and filled." He stopped. He noticed. He got involved. He sat with the grieving. He touched the diseased. He knelt beside the forgotten. That is what real love looks like.

And if we are to follow Him, we must resist the cultural pull toward detachment. Real ministry does not happen through a screen. It happens in living rooms, on curbsides, in waiting rooms, and in awkward silences and wet tears. It happens when we choose to *stay*, rather than scroll.

Not long ago, I met a teenager at a church I was helping. On the surface, he was bright, polite, and very involved. He smiled all the time. But behind his eyes, I sensed something dark and unspoken lingering.

So, one day, I asked if we could talk. We sat together in a quiet, open room. I shared a bit of my story and told him, "If you ever need someone safe to talk to, I will be that person."

Something shifted in his eyes. Hesitantly, he began to open up. He told me how, as a child, an older neighbor had exposed himself and pressured him to pull down his pants. He did not go along with it; he ran and told his mother. But the shame lingered. The confusion did not fade with time; it distorted how he saw himself. He began to question his sexuality. He had never told anyone until that day.

I did not lecture him. I did not try to fix it. I simply listened and thanked him for trusting me. From that day forward, he knew he had a friend and a safe place. Someone who would not judge or gossip. Someone who would simply be there.

That is what ministry looks like more often than we think. Not miracles or microphones, but showing up with open ears when someone does not know where else to turn. Presence is a radical act in a world trained to disengage. It costs time. It costs emotional energy. It asks us to slow down when everything around us says, "Keep moving."

When you choose to sit with someone who is falling apart, when you hold the hand of someone who has no words left, you are showing them the heart of Jesus.

He did not look down on us with sympathy. He came down. Felt our grief. Tasted our rejection. Endured our sorrow. He still meets us in the middle of our mess. And now, He sends us to do the same.

When you step away from your comfort zone and into someone else's chaos, you are becoming the hands and feet of Christ. So, ask yourself: Am I watching suffering from a distance... or walking into it with Him?

THE LEGACY OF A COMFORT-GIVER

One day, people will speak about the life you lived. What will they say? Will they recall a trail of blessings or simply a trail of busyness? Will your presence leave behind the fragrance of peace... or only the dust of hurried indifference?

Every moment we choose to meet someone where they are. Every conversation. Every interruption we allow. These are the acts that shape our legacy, not only in the eyes of people, but in the eyes of God.

Isaiah paints a beautiful picture of this legacy: *"How beautiful upon the mountains are the feet of him that bringeth good tidings, that publisheth peace; that bringeth good tidings of good, that publisheth salvation; that saith unto Zion, Thy God reigneth!"* (Isaiah 52:7)

Your life can carry good news of salvation, peace, and hope. Most often, that does not happen from a pulpit. It happens on Skid Row. In a grief-stricken kitchen. In a prison visitation area. In a place where someone has not laughed in months. That is where the gospel enters suffering hearts.

And when you go to those places, you will find that ministry does not simply flow through you; it transforms you. Time after time, I have stepped into another's pain believing I was there to serve... only to find God serving me. My wounds were softened. My blind spots were revealed. My grasp of His mercy was expanded. God uses us to reach others, but He also uses others to reach us.

You do not have to be whole to be helpful. You only need to be willing, surrendered, and available. Because it is often the cracks in your own life that become channels of grace for someone else.

And when you walk away from those sacred moments, you know this is what you were made for. That is a legacy worth remembering.

IN HELPING OTHERS, GOD HELPS YOU

One of the most surprising blessings about helping others is how deeply it ends up helping us.

It almost seems backward. You would expect that pouring into someone else while you are still healing would leave you empty. You would expect that walking through another's grief would only drain your already-tired heart. But mysteriously and beautifully, God meets us in the giving.

"Give, and it shall be given unto you," Jesus said (Luke 6:38). That promise is not limited to money or possessions; it reaches into the comfort of another person's presence, compassion, and shared sorrow.

The way of Jesus is a sacred exchange: giving and receiving, pouring out and being filled. He tends our wounds as we care for the wounds of others, and in the act of comforting, we find comfort quietly flourishing within our own souls.

Romans 12:15 unveils more of the heart behind this: *"Rejoice with them that do rejoice, and weep with them that weep."* This is not merely a suggestion; it is an invitation. It describes the life of a Christian community. Joy multiplies when it is shared. Sorrow lightens when someone else helps bear it.

When you walk with someone through their troubles—not as a fixer, but as a friend—you are stepping into the heart of Christ Himself. You are obeying the call to *love your neighbor as thyself* (Matthew 22:39).

The more we live this way—slowing down, noticing pain, choosing to stay—the more we discover Jesus not only as our personal Saviour but as the ever-present Companion in every act of love, every burden shared, every tear embraced.

When you show up to help others, you may be thinking, *I hope I can encourage them*. But more often, you walk away realizing: *God encouraged me, too*. Because in carrying another's burden, you uncover how close Christ truly is. And that nearness does not fade. It lingers, strengthens, and becomes part of who you are.

SENT INTO THE WORLD WITH HIS COMFORT

If you have made it this far in life, then you have walked through valleys, endured wilderness seasons, stared grief in the face, wrestled with questions that refused easy answers, and carried burdens that no one else could fully understand. And yet, here you are, still reaching, hoping, and believing that somehow, God is doing something with all of this. And He is. Even when you could not see it, He was shaping you, softening what had grown hard, and strengthening what had felt so fragile.

And now, on the other side of sorrow, you are not just someone who survived. You are someone with something to give. Because every wound Christ has comforted, every tear He has caught, every long night that did not undo you was not wasted. It was preparation.

God never lets pain pass through your life without purpose. From ashes, He creates beauty (Isaiah 61:3). From sorrow, He births compassion. And He places a calling in your hands to be present with others. So, go and step into someone else's storm. Be the eyes that truly see. The voice that speaks life. The arms that hold steady. The feet that walk with the weary.

You do not have to fix everything. You simply have to show up. And when you do, you carry Christ with you. You get to represent

Christ to others who are in pain and suffering. Every time you choose love when it would be easier to look away, you preach the gospel in a way no sermon ever could.

You are not disqualified because you have been broken. You are qualified because you have been redeemed.

Every act of grace, every moment of presence, and every trembling prayer shared is holy and eternal. They are echoes of Calvary and a foretaste of Heaven.

This is what you were made for. To love the LORD with all your heart, to love your neighbor as yourself, and to bring Christ's hope into a hurting world. So, let's thank Him, not only for the healing, but for the calling that came through the suffering.

Let's praise the LORD who walked with us through the fire and who never turned away. Who still loves us today, tomorrow, and for all eternity without end. Jesus Christ is faithful. Jesus is good. And Jesus is with you—always.

DEAR FRIEND,

Writing this book was never simply an exercise in words. It was born prayerfully from real conversations, tears, and deep reflection with those who are walking through their own suffering. My hope has been simple: that somewhere in these pages, you have felt seen, understood, and reminded that Christ is near, even in the darkest places.

Many people have confidentially shared with me their own stories of loss, grief, betrayal, injustice, and honest questions about faith. I have found that some of the most meaningful healing happens not in isolation, but in safe spaces where pain can be spoken aloud and met with compassion, truth, and the hope we have in Jesus Christ.

My desire is to exalt the Lord and to serve others with the same comfort I have received from Him. It has been a privilege to listen, to learn, and to walk alongside others as we seek God's wisdom together in the dark valleys of life.

Because of this, God has allowed me to serve people in many places by speaking on the subject of suffering, offering conferences, workshops, and times of teaching and open conversation centered on seasons of deep pain and discovering God's sustaining grace. If you sense these themes could serve your church, ministry, or gathering, you are warmly welcome to reach out. Any invitation would be approached prayerfully and with a genuine desire to serve in whatever way would be most helpful.

You may contact me through the ministry's website at www.MissionFrontier.info. May Christ be preeminent in all matters, and may His grace be embraced abundantly in every season.

In the service of Christ,

Lawrence Bowman

Other Books for the Journey

If you've found comfort in this book, you may also be
interested in these other works by Lawrence Bowman:

Determined:
to have life more abundantly

Confessions:
A Memoir of Hope for the Suffering

Left Alive

Voices Against
Sex Slavery in America

Order your copies at:
amazon • MissionFrontier.info • WaymakerPubishing.com

Stories for Little Hearts

Children's books available in English & Spanish

Written to encourage kindness
and hope—one story at a time.

These stories are available in both English and Spanish.

The Soulwinning Series

A four-book series equipping Christians to use ordinary life for extraordinary gospel impact—through witness, influence, and discipleship.

A Practical Approach in Doing the Great Commission

Lawrence Bowman

Practical and Effective Methods for Sharing the Gospel

And [Jesus] said unto them, Go ye into all the world, and preach the gospel to every creature. And that repentance and remission of sins should be preached in his name among all nations, beginning at Jerusalem.
— Mark 16:15, Luke 24:47

Lawrence Bowman

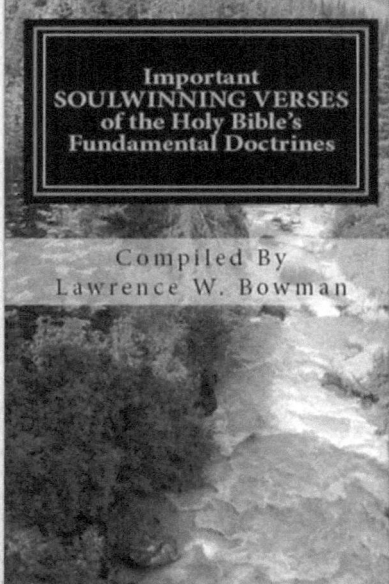

Important SOULWINNING VERSES of the Holy Bible's Fundamental Doctrines

Compiled By Lawrence W. Bowman

A Simple Understanding of the Great Commission

SOULWINNING02   Lawrence Bowman